This is a kin

THE FOURTH DIMENSION
Dani Dedeaux

ADMISSIONS

Destiny & Joyce Marie,
You have no idea how losing you has impacted me. Not only did it break me, it remolded me. Continue resting beautifully.
I love you x a million.

Lulu & Mags,
Thank you for seeing the vision beyond what I could. For always pushing me to create. For never giving up on my dream even when I wanted to.

Kenni + Savvy,
You know you light up my sky and fill my lungs,
Thank you for helping me keep my imagination alive.

COMPENDIUM
I: PROLEGOMENON
II: CARCANET
III: CONTEMPTIBLE
IV: ASSEMBLAGE
V: ATTAINMENT
VI: AMOUR PROPRE
VII: ONEIRISM
VIII: OVERTURES
IX: BDSR
X: INAUGURATE
XI: BEGUILED
XII: KVETCHING
XIII: INIQUITIOUS
XIV: COMMISERATION
XVI: DENOUEMENT

I: PROLEGOMENON

"Come on Xena, you have to come." Sarai begged as we walked into Biology.

"I don't think it's a good idea, S." I sat down at my desk. "It's just not for me."

"Why not?" She whined. "You never come."

"Hello class! Guess what we'll be dissecting today!" Mr. Groves walked in with his big metal cart of terror.

Mr. Groves' instructions always came with a twist so you had to pay close attention. Especially when it came to dissection day. As soon as the cart passes by your table, your partner is supposed to quickly grab a tray or else you'd both instantly fail the assignment. The mystery tray came with gloves, two masks and something horrid inside. Thankfully, it was my partner Casey's turn and she was always quick.

"What do you think it is this time?" I frowned as we put on our gear.

"Knowing Mr. Groves, probably a cow brain!" She shrieked.

"Don't touch your trays yet!" He ordered.

"I have a question!" Lisa raised her hand.

Lisa was the classic frenemy. That one really pretty girl that bullied her way to the number one spot. She was cruel, sneaky and self-centered. The complete opposite of her twin, Lydia, who was one of my closest friends. I could play nice with Lisa, but I knew that I could *never* trust her.

"Yes Ms. Samuels?" He sighed deeply as she stood up.

"I just don't understand why we have to be an all-girls school and also, these uniforms are not it." She complained.

Unfortunately for us, she complained about those two things every day. I personally liked the uniform. It was simple. Black high waisted skirts and a tucked plain shirt with our school logo on it. It was supposed to be a punishment that went along with the new anti-bullying system. They figured if we all dressed the same, the problems would fade away but being in high school, girls always found new ways to tease each other.

"That's not a question." He parked the cart in the back of the class and walked to the front.

"I know but-"

"Can we just stick to Biology, please?" He rubbed his temples.

"Fine." She plopped back down in her seat.

"Okay class." He rubbed his hands together excitedly. "Open your—"

"Wait! I didn't get a tray!" Lisa shouted.

"You know what that means." He hid his smirk. "See you Monday."

"But-" She whined.

"But nothing. See you Monday." He said seriously. "Maybe next time you'll pay attention."

"Fine. I need to get a mani-pedi anyway." She gathered her things.

"You losers better be at the spot at 7." She looked at us before walking out.

"Anyway girls." He sat on the edge of his desk. "Let's continue."

We all sat there hesitant to touch our assignments.

"Do the honors." I slid the tray over to Casey.

"No thank you." She slid it back in front of me.

Lying in the middle of the tray was an organ that reeked of rotting flesh.

I looked back at my friends Lydia and Zoe who didn't seem to care about the assignment. They sat there nonchalantly flipping through catalogs. I was the only one in our friend group that actually cared about school.

"What is it?" Casey poked at it with tongs.

"It's a cow heart." Mr. G smiled.

"Gross!" Lydia whined.

"If you can turn this beautifully crafted organ into a chocolate heart, you can leave early." He folded his arms.

"Should be simple." Casey nudged me.

"Super easy." I smirked.

After a moment of studying the organ, I could see the girls around me start to crumble.

"I can't do this." A girl across the room complained. "I'll take the F."

"Fine." He shrugged. "Anyone else?"

"Actually." Zoe started to raise her hand.

"Seriously?" I scowled at her.

"Never mind." She awkwardly dropped her hand.

"Get started, girls." He grabbed the Witch Weekly magazine from his desk and flipped it open.

"So, the spell for this should be in the back of the book." Casey sighed.

"Well." I flipped through it. "I think it's somewhere in the middle."

"Help us!" Zoe and Lydia whispered.

"Sorry, we want to finish first. You'll have to wait." I smirked.

"My bet is still on the back of the book." Casey watched me.

"It's actually right – here!" I pointed to the spell.

"Damn." She groaned.

"You owe me lunch." I smirked.

Casey and I were lab partners but I also considered her a friend. The girls didn't like me hanging out with her, mostly because Lisa convinced them that she wasn't cool enough. But, I hung out with who I wanted.

I highlighted the spell and grabbed her hand.

We closed our eyes and quietly whispered it. When we opened them, there was a big chocolate heart plastered on our desk.

"Great job Team Casanova!" Mr. G shouted. "You are the first to finish. You may take your candy heart and go."

Mr. Groves had us broken up into teams of two for the year and gave us quirky little nicknames. We were the Casanovas, while Lydia and Zoe were the Heartbreak Babies. He was very much obsessed with human romance.

"Yes." We high-fived happily.

"Congratulations." Zoe muttered.

"Here crybaby." I turned to face her.

I flipped through the pages of her book with the power of my finger. I stopped on the page and smiled at her.

"Thanks, X." Lydia smiled.

"Xena." Mr. G cleared his throat.

"Yes?" I turned around hoping he couldn't see the guilt on my face.

"You girls can go now." He said again.

"Actually I wanted to stay and watch if that's okay?" I smiled at him.

"That's fine." He shoved his face back in the magazine.

Casey and I sat there whispering and watching everyone struggle.

"Screw this." Reagan whispered as she stood up.

Reagan was very standoffish and unapproachable. She was usually Lisa's lab partner but due to Lisa's absence, she had to work alone to get the grade she deserved. Lesson one, never piss off an introvert. She pulled her wand from her boot and kept it hidden at her side.

"Don't do it." I whispered to her.

"Shut up." She looked back at me.

I watched as the hands of the clock began to spin rapidly, until the clock landed at 4:55. I sat there in shock as she bowed proudly. Everyone stood up and started to pack up.

"What are you doing?" Mr. G looked away from his magazine.

"Packing up." A girl said proudly. "It's time to go."

"Nonsense. It's only what? 11:30?" He looked down at his watch.

"You sure about that?" She replied.

"Yes." He hesitated as he turned to face the clock on the wall.
"Okay, who did it?"

"Did what, Mr. G?" Reagan smirked.

"The time, Reagan." He folded his arms.

"But why would someone do that?" She pulled off her gloves.

"She's dead meat." Zoe whispered.

"What was that?" His eyes locked on Zoe.

"Nothing." She shook her head.

He pulled his wand from his desk and pointed it at her. He spun it around in circles and we watched Zoe's mouth move with it, as if he was rewinding her. When he stopped his wand, her mouth stopped moving too.

"Now to turn it up." He pointed his wand in the air three times. "And play."

"She's dead meat." Zoe repeated loudly.

"Ah, thank you Heartbreak Babies." He smiled.

"*Babies?* I didn't say anything." Lydia corrected him.

"Well, you work together. You are a team." He explained.

"Of course." She rolled her eyes.

"Now either someone is going to tell me who did it or all of you, outside of the Casanova's of course, will have night school." He threatened.

"What?" Zoe panicked. "I can't miss tonight."

"Me either." Lydia murmured.

Everyone started to quietly complain because they all had plans to go to the meeting tonight.

"Reagan did it." Everyone admitted at the same time.

"Thanks guys. Way to hold out." She frowned.

"See, was that so hard?" He waved his hand and the door flung open. "Have a nice spring break everyone."

We all rushed to the door and into the hallways.

"Except you Reagan." He closed the door and trapped her inside.

Three weeks off only gave me time to handle everything with college. I didn't get to have fun like everyone else. Applications and acceptance letters were all that mattered to my parents.

"What's gonna happen?" I asked as we continued down the hallway.

"I think it's safe to say we won't see her at the WGW tonight." Sarai smirked.

"Who cares?" Zoe cheered. "It's spring break!"

"Where's Isis?" I looked around.

"I don't know but I see Lisa. Later." Lydia rushed over to her sister.

"Please come tonight!" Sarai begged me again.

"I just – I can't. Even if I wanted to." I frowned.

"We'll talk about this on the way home." She avowed.

"So, you're coming over?" I smirked.

"This conversation is far from over." She emptied her backpack into the trash.

"Let's go then." I shoved my books in my locker and slammed it shut.

"You can't miss the party for Zaria. It's literally a holiday." She continued.

"Yeah, I know." I sighed.

Zaria Dixon was the witch who made it possible for us to be taught about the four other dimensions. The WGW was a place where all dimensions could meet up secretly, hosted by us – the fourth dimension. There were three young leaders of each dimension that came together to throw these epic parties. But what Sarai didn't understand was the reason why I could never step foot in there. There were laws in place. Laws that were very simple and mandatory to follow. We were not to have any communication with beings outside of our dimension, and unlike my friends, I had no choice but to honor that. My father was the Mayor and was set to be the new ruler of our dimension, while my mother sat on the board of Witchman. Witchman controlled our education system. They were the ones who told us what was safe to learn and what was forbidden. They made all the rules and decided our punishments. If I went, my parents' positions of power would be at risk and I couldn't see them suffer just because I wanted to be a selfish little girl and party with my friends. I couldn't say that I wasn't tempted though.

"So, Xena." Lisa and her minions blocked my exit.

"What?" I sighed.

"Leave her alone, Lisa." Sarai stepped in front of me.

"She can speak for herself, guard dog." She said rudely.

"It's okay, S." I put my hand on her shoulder.

"Cute." She smirked. "So, are you going or not?"

"You know the answer to that already." I rolled my eyes.

"Why are you so chicken shit?" She crossed her arms.

"Isis!" I pushed past Lisa.

"X!" She hugged me. "Is it me or did school go by like, really fast?"

"You can thank Reagan." Sarai smirked.

"Mm. I've always liked that girl." Isis grinned.

"Let's go home." We linked arms and walked out of the double doors.

"What's for lunch Veronica?" I asked as we walked into my kitchen.

Veronica was my childhood nanny. My parents brought her back from the human dimension to do all the things they couldn't. My father said she would be like a second mother to me and that she would take care of me when my parents were unavailable, which was all the time but I didn't mind at all. Truthfully, we were closer than my parents and I ever were. She was more relaxed when we were alone and very structured when they were around. I liked that about her. I liked that I could be normal around her. She was in her mid-20's and was beyond beautiful. She had short shaggy brown hair and a body that anyone would envy. She looked like a model from one of those human magazines Father liked to hide from Mother and me.

"Watercress sandwiches and cucumber slices." She looked at me.

"Gross." Isis groaned as we sat down at the bar.

"Let me guess." I sighed.

"Your Father is having guests over the house for a lunch meeting and that is what they requested." She explained.

"What's for dinner then?" I grabbed a banana from the fruit bowl.

"Beef wellington with sautéed brussels sprouts." She smirked.

"Yes to the wellington, hold the sprouts." Sarai instructed.

"Oh, I didn't know you three would be staying for dinner." She frowned.

"Why wouldn't we be?" I spun around in the chair.

"Well, Mr. Briarwood made it clear that it was a guest only invite and with all due respect you are family." She intentionally avoided eye contact.

"Ouch." Isis whispered.

"So I get kicked out of my own house for the night?" I chuckled dryly. "What am I supposed to do? Where am I supposed to go?"

Isis and Sarai looked at each other and back at me.

"No." I shook my head. I already knew what they were thinking.

"Come on, X!" Isis whined.

"No." I walked out of the kitchen with my hands over my ears.

"Xena!" Isis chased me up the stairs. "Come on!"

"No!" I yelled back.

I ran into the hallway closet and hid. Hide and go seek was played a little differently in our dimension. I quickly shrunk myself and jumped into an empty flower pot. It reeked of old dirt and worms. I plugged my nose and waited for her to find me.

"Where did she go?" Sarai said out of breath. "This house is too damn big to search."

"Give me a second. I know her every hiding spot." Isis promised.

I listened closely to their footsteps going in the opposite direction.

"Ha!" Isis snatched the door open.

"Told you nothing was in here." Sarai pouted.

"Wait." Isis' voice got closer.

The pot began to move and I could see Isis' face above me. She was holding the pot in her hands. I held my laugh and braced myself for the fall.

"What are you going to do with that?" Sarai asked, puzzled. "Hit her with it?"

"Not exactly." She laughed.

She let the pot hit the ground and shatter. I returned to my original size as soon as I touched the ground.

"Hey." I whined as I shook the dirt from my hair.

"How did you know she would be in there?" Sarai smiled.

"I know my best friend." She helped me up. "She's been hiding there since we were 5."

"Not fair." I dusted off my pants with a smile.

"Will you go now?" Isis pinned me against the wall.

"You're trapped now." Sarai laughed deviously behind her.

I impulsively licked Isis' face but she didn't budge.

"You were supposed to get freaked out." I frowned.

"Not that easily." She smiled.

"Come on X. Just go. What will it hurt?" Sarai sighed.

"I would be grounded until I was dead." I explained.

"How? It works. Your parents have guests coming over. You have to be out of the house anyway. You can just sneak over to the WG warehouse and then say you are spending the night at my house. My parents are out of town for the weekend. Come on." Isis begged.

"I – I don't know." I hesitated. "Me and lies don't mix well."

"When's the last time you told a lie, Xena?" Sarai scoffed.

"Was that rhetorical?" I sighed.

"Exactly. One lie won't hurt you." Isis shrugged. "And technically you *are* spending the night at my house. You're just leaving out one minor detail."

"Seems pretty major to me." I said sarcastically.

"What they don't know won't hurt them." She sang.

"You're right, it'll kill them." I sighed.

"Please, X. Pretty please." She whined. "Just this once."

"We'll never ask again." Sarai begged.

"Fine." I sighed.

"Really?" Her eyes lit up.

"Never mind the reconfirmation! Let's get you ready before you change your mind!" Isis pulled me into my room.

II: CARCANET

"You are *not* wearing that." Sarai laughed.

"Why not?" I looked down at my outfit.

I was wearing my usual button up and loose slacks. It was the attire that my parents had picked out for me. I wasn't allowed to wear anything else. They had my outfits picked out by the week. And it was all that I knew and what I was comfortable in.

"No offense, but you look like you are headed to a meeting with the president." She frowned.

"Actually, I wore this to election day." I smiled proudly.

"You say that like it's a good thing." She muttered.

"Shut up, S." Isis walked into my closet.

She was in there for a few minutes and came back with a handful of clothes I'd never seen before.

"What's all that?" I stared at the pile.

"It's what you are wearing tonight." She shoved it in a duffle bag.

"Can I see it?" I tried to peek in the bag.

"No." She zipped it. "If you can't see it, you can't change it."

"So, I'm getting dressed at your house?" I sighed.

"Wouldn't want your parents to see you wearing this." She winked.

"Great." I groaned.

"Let's go." She walked out of my room.

I grabbed my phone from my nightstand and shoved it in my pocket.

"I never understood why your parents don't let you bring your phone to school." Sarai fixed her hair in the mirror.

"I have to stay focused, my phone will only distract me." I mocked my father.

"Lame." She made a kissy face in the mirror and walked out.

"Yeah, I guess it is." I said to myself as I followed.

"Hello girls." My mother greeted us when we reached the bottom of the stairs.

"Hello Mother." I smiled.

My mother was a tall brunette with a short curly bob. She had the most beautiful brown eyes and the softest facial features. She was everything I wanted to look like. I remember when I was younger she used to laugh a lot and take me places – just the two of us. Now she only laughs if we're in a meeting with a potential client or to appease my father. She doesn't take me anywhere anymore either, she just takes trips across the dimensions and brings me a souvenir with a horrible backstory. I would do anything to see my mother genuinely smile again. She is just like my father now. He doesn't laugh – he doesn't smile. We have no conversation unless it has to do with college or his career. We have no bond. We have no relationship.

"Where are you three headed?" She slipped out of her shoes.

"To Isis' house." I promised her.

"You heard about your fathers' meeting didn't you?" She pulled her hair from its perfect bun.

"Yes, that's why we are leaving. I'm just going to spend the night over there." I said nervously.

"And what are you girls going to be doing tonight?" She smirked.

"Uh." I looked over at Isis.

"Just staying in." Isis lied, "My mom's going to rent some movies for us and get a whole bunch of snacks. Have a girl's night in."

"That sounds perfect." Mother sounded pleased. "Enjoy."

"We will. Thanks Mother." I said as I pushed Sarai to walk.

As we walked out the door my mother called my name.

"Yes Mother?" I looked back at her.

"Don't eat too much, we wouldn't want you to be bloated for the festivities on Monday." She smiled.

"We're actually throwing that this year?" I pretended to be excited.

"Yes, your Father wouldn't have it any other way." She said through her teeth. "So I need you girls to help out Sunday night and Monday morning. This house will be hectic for the next couple of days."

"Yes Mother." I walked out.

"I can't believe I'm doing this." I whined as we walked down my front steps.

"You'll be fine." Isis promised.

"You're just lucky you live next door to me or else she wouldn't have let me go." I chuckled dryly.

"Funny how things work out, huh?" She winked. "Pays to be the goddaughter."

"That's so true cause you're literally *never* allowed at my house." Sarai pouted.

"That's because you have all brothers." I laughed. "My mom would be a fool to let me go there."

Isis lived in a house a little smaller than mine but it felt more like home than mine ever could. Even when it was empty. It was dressed in warm colors and the fireplace was always burning gingerbread scented wood. The house was decorated with pictures of Isis and her sister. I was the only one in our friend group that was an only child but they never failed to make me feel like a part of their family. The closest thing I had to a sister was my older cousin Catarina but I rarely saw her anymore. She moved to Beauclair, where the WG warehouse was located. She was one of the founders along with Lisa and Leslie's older sister Layla.

"Time to get dressed." Isis said excitedly as we walked in her room. "Sarai you get dressed in my left closet, Xena you get dressed in my right, and I'll get dressed out here. We'll surprise each other."

"Okay." I forced a smile as I grabbed the duffle bag from her.

"I'll just find something in your closet." Sarai walked away.

"Go on." Isis shooed me into the closet.

I walked in my designated changing room and closed the door. I opened the duffle bag and slowly pulled out the outfit.

I slipped on the clothes and stared at myself in her mirror. She picked out a strawberry-red and blue plaid cashmere sweater with ripped blue jeans that exposed my hips and her red high-tops. I surprisingly liked how I looked but if my parents caught me in this, I would be banished to my room until I graduated from college. It was all about appearances with them. At least she grabbed my favorite perfume. It was the most expensive bottle in the human dimension. My father got it for me a couple of weeks ago and I've been addicted to it ever since.

"Come on out girls!" Isis yelled.

I took a deep breath and slowly opened the door.

"Wow. I did good." Isis looked me up and down. "You look great."

"Really?" I said nervously as I stepped out.

"Yes. Now breathe." She turned back to her vanity.

"Wow me? Wow you." I stared at her.

"Thanks Babe." She smirked.

It was no surprise that Isis looked beautiful. She was perfect even when she woke up in the morning. She had long blonde hair and big green eyes. Her body was sculpted perfectly.

She was wearing a black skirt and this season's floral crop top. Her stomach was completely exposed. Her belly button piercing dangled over her skirt.

"Where'd you get these? I've never seen them before." I looked down.

"Remember when I stayed at your house for a week when my parents left for the human dimension?" She applied her lipstick.

"Yeah." I nodded.

"I left some of my clothes over there that I never got back from you." She smiled. "But the cashmere is yours."

"I figured." I chuckled.

"Sarai!" Isis yelled as she blotted her lips.

"Coming." Sarai opened the door.

I looked back at her and she was wearing a tight black dress and flats. She kept her hair in a tight bun so that her neck would be exposed. She had a beautiful neck and even better collarbones. She knew that. She was complimented on the two very often.

"Beautiful." Isis smiled.

"Why are you getting so dressed up?" I watched her.

"I have a boy to see." Sarai smiled.

"A boy from another dimension?" I gasped.

"Yes." She nodded.

"That's illegal. You know that right?" I walked over to her.

"I'm aware." She scoffed.

"Can you do her makeup?" Isis interrupted us.

"Sure." Sarai grabbed the make up bag from the vanity and pulled me over to the bed.

"I don't wear makeup." I refused.

"Not too much, but not too little." Isis ordered Sarai.

"Gotcha." She put the brush to my face.

I sat there nervous and not even breathing. I wondered what I was going to look like and what my parents would think If I got caught like this. I started to second guess myself.

"Stop it, X." Isis ordered as she stood to her feet.

"What?" I said trying to keep my eyes open for the eyeliner.

"You're overthinking it." She shook her head.

"I'm not." I forced a smile.

"I thought you never lied?" Sarai smirked.

"Okay, I am." I sighed.

"Stop. It'll be fine." Isis promised.

"All done." Sarai stood up.

"X." Isis smirked.

"What?" I asked frantically.

"See for yourself." She passed me a mirror.

My jaw dropped as I studied myself. I looked completely different – I looked *beautiful.* Older. I looked daring and just as stunning as they did. I couldn't stop looking at myself. I was completely shocked by my quick transformation.

"We should upload a picture to Witchspace." Sarai suggested.

"Bad idea." Isis shook her head. "X wouldn't want her parents to see her like this."

I took one more look at myself and shrugged. If anything I would just say we were playing around in Isis' make-up.

"Take the picture, S." I smiled.

We posed for the picture and she uploaded it before I could change my mind. This was the first time I didn't go crazy over the possibilities and I was kinda excited for everyone to see the new me.

"Okay, we gotta go." Isis grabbed her purse.

"You're forgetting something." I frowned.

"What?" She sighed.

"My hair." I pointed to my messy bun.

"Oh shoot, come here." She pulled my hair from its bun and my curls fell past my shoulders.

"A little hair spray and you're perfect." She smiled as she sprayed it.

"There." She tossed the can and pulled me to my feet.

"Okay, let's go then." I grabbed my purse.

"Well, look at you all eager now." Sarai laughed.

"Whatever." I looked at myself one more time and walked out.

"This shall be fun." Isis said behind me.

As soon as we entered the town of Beauclair, I instantly smiled. The town was so much brighter and filled with color. The beings were friendly and there were kids playing outside. Beauclair was considered middle class while Oxenfurt – where I lived – was considered high class. The classes occasionally mixed but it wasn't likely for you to have friends of a different class *and* be accepted socially. It was broken down into sections. Middle and lower, and Upper-middle and higher. I hated it. I hated the fact that we could only hang out with those who were of the same level of wealth. That was why I barely saw Catarina because even though she came from a family of money, she was now considered middle class and was denied access to come through the gates of Oxenfurt.

"Almost there." Isis said excitedly.

"I'm going to puke." I whined.

"Out the window at least." She rubbed my shoulder.

"No you are not. Throwing up means crying and no way you are messing up my masterpiece." Sarai said with a smile.

"I just don't know what to expect or how to act." I murmured.

"Just be you." Isis smiled.

"No, do not be you." Sarai interjected.

"Why not?" Isis looked at her rudely.

"Be someone else. *Anyone* else. Pretend as if you are someone else. Pretend to be middle class. You can even have a fake name. You can be Tina. But do not be yourself – don't get me wrong I love who you are. It's just easier to be someone else here and your parents can't track you by name or personality. You can actually be free here." She explained.

"Isis?" I looked for her approval.

"She's kind of right." She admitted.

"Don't worry." Sarai promised me.

"Nyomi it is." I grinned.

"Nyomi? Isn't that your middle name?" Sarai asked, confused.

"But technically it wouldn't be a lie it's still her name." Isis explained.

"Loopholes, I like it." Sarai said proudly.

Isis understood me in ways I could never explain. I didn't have to explain it though because she knew. She knew everything about me, from the time I was born to my deepest darkest secrets. She was how a sister should be.

"We're here." She shrieked as we pulled up to an abandoned warehouse.

"No one's here." I looked around confused.

"Yes they are." Sarai smiled.

"No, they aren't. There are no cars here." I snarled. "Is this a joke?"

"Wait for it." Isis chuckled.

I sat there quietly waiting for whatever was supposed to happen to actually happen. I watched Isis as we carefully parked.

"Why are you being so careful?" I whispered.

"Shh." She pressed her finger to my lips.

"Okay, okay." I shrugged her off.

"Let's go girls." She got out.

I heard a slam as if Sarai's door hit another car.

"Sarai, seriously?" Isis asked angrily.

"Sorry I couldn't see how close we were." She said apologetically.

"Pay attention." Isis scolded her.

"Okay you two have officially lost it." I stepped out of the car.

As we walked over to the building, I felt goosebumps rise all over my body.

"Play it cool." Sarai slid her crystal necklace on.

"We will still be here." Isis promised.

"What do you mean?" I tried to hide my panic.

"Just watch." Isis slid on her necklace too.

And there I was alone, in front of this dark abandoned building.

"Where are you guys?" I panicked.

"Here." Isis touched my shoulder.

A swift knock on the door sent it flying open.

"Hey girls." A boy's voice greeted us.

"Hey Sam." I could hear the smile in Isis' voice.

"Who's the tenderfoot?" He asked playfully.

"The tender what?" I asked confused.

"This is Xe- I mean, Nyomi." She laughed.

"Hello Nyomi." He addressed me.

"I would shake your hand, if I could see you." I smiled uncomfortably.

"I can fix that." Floating crystal came towards me.

"Whoa." I jumped as I felt something around my neck.

"It's just me." He laughed in my ear.

"Oh." I chuckled uncomfortably.

The necklace began to glow and the girls appeared at my side again. Isis had her flirty eyes on and Sarai was staring at me. I turned around to see the lot full of cars.

"Is that better?" He smiled.

"Way better." I nodded.

He was cute. He had dark brown hair and his smile was invigorating. The way Isis was looking, she had her name written all over him, but I really wanted to see who Sarai was crushing on.

"One rule, you can talk to anyone you want to but no love interest from other dimensions. That is forbidden." He smiled at Isis then back at me. "Do you understand?"

"Yes." I nodded sincerely.

"Come on in." He moved away from the door.

"Thank you." I smiled as I stepped in.

Inside looked completely different than the outside. It was decked out like an arcade. There were different levels. The bottom floor was a lounge room. There were 12 empty kings and queens chairs on a podium. I assumed that's where the founders sat. The second floor was archery, third floor was sword fighting, the fourth floor was the witch-off floor and the fifth floor I couldn't see yet but I was excited to explore them all.

"This is amazing." I smiled.

"Overwhelming though huh?" Sam placed his hand on my shoulder.

"Yes actually." I looked at his hand.

"So, Sam." Isis started. "Wanna go with me to grab the programs?"

"Oh, sure." He smiled.

They disappeared and I was left with Sarai who was clearly on the look out for someone.

"What's his name?" I smiled.

"Josh." She smiled back.

"If you're looking for the 3rd dimension they aren't here yet." Lisa walked up behind us. "Xena?"

"It's Nyomi." Sarai hissed.

"Nyomi." She crossed her arms. "You came."

"Yeah, I did." I smiled.

"Guess you aren't a prude after all." She admitted.

"Guess not." I rolled my eyes.

"You look – nice." She stormed off.

"Wow, I think L just gave you a compliment." Sarai smirked.

"Sarai!" Lydia embraced her.

"X?" She pulled away to look at me. "I can't believe you're actually here."

"Yeah, I know." I whispered.

"You look beautiful." She smiled.

"Hey guys, hey Nyomi." Zoe walked up behind us.

"Finally someone that can play along." I hugged her.

"Yeah Isis texted me and filled me in." She hugged me back. "I like it."

"Where is Isis?" Lydia looked around.

"She's in the bathroom." I lied.

"Did she say bathroom? She meant the backroom with Sam." Sarai blurted.

"If she gets caught she-"

"Alright I love you guys but I gotta go find someone." Lydia walked away.

"Me too actually." Sarai followed after her.

"And then there were two." I smiled at Zoe.

"Let's go find somewhere to sit. The other dimensions should be coming any minute now." She pulled me through the crowd.

"Since we are practically family we get to sit closest to the founders." She bragged as we sat down on the swinging love seat.

"Cool." I smiled.

"Here they come." She pointed to the opening door.

"Who?" I asked, looking down at my shoes to avoid any eye contact.

"The 3rd dimension. My personal favorite." She said proudly.

"Where's the other dimensions?" I whispered.

"1st is always fashionably late." She chuckled dryly. "*Humans.*"

"And 2nd?" I asked, making conversation.

"Probably feeding in the woods." She shrugged. "We supply them with food."

"You say that so calmly." I looked at her.

"You know me. The subtler the better." She grinned. "Look at them."

"Why are they so flawless?" I whined as they walked through.

They looked like perfectly sculpted statues, not a flaw in sight. They moved so gently yet with force. I could feel the hair on the back of my neck rising.

"They're vampires. They *are* perfect." She sighed.

"They are so pale." I smiled.

"Yeah, the paleness is definitely attractive." She laughed. "Don't stare so hard."

"Right." I looked back down at the ground as they walked past us.

"There's your cousin." She pointed to Catarina from across the room.

"Great, I hope she doesn't point me out." I groaned.

The lights dimmed and I looked around as everyone rushed to take their seats.

"What's happening?" I whispered.

"1st and 2nd have arrived. That means we are going to start soon." She said excitedly.

I watched out of the corner of my eye as the founders took their seats.

"Do you smell that?" I held my nose.

"Does it smell like, wet dog?" She whispered.

"Yes." I said disgustedly.

"That'll be the 2nd dimension." She chuckled.

"We supply them with food, can we bathe them too?" I teased.

"I wish." She nudged me.

A loud voice came over the intercom silencing all side conversations.

"Welcome to the WGW, formerly known as the dimensional games. To all the familiar faces, welcome back and to our new members, congratulations! I couldn't think of a better way for you to spend your Friday night. Let's quickly go over a few things for the newcomers; The twelve beings you see before you are your superiors. And before you ask, yes, all of them. Three beings from each dimension. Treat them equally. Also, before you start wandering off, you *must* mingle with at least one superior from outside your dimension. You are to ask them a simple question like, their name and what they like to do. You may also go to them for advice or information. Everyone here is your friend — However, we have one rule that cannot be broken under any circumstances. There will be no love connections to be made while in the WGW. If we catch you, you will be banned indefinitely along with a series of consequences.

Other than that, enjoy your night and let the games begin!"

Everyone stood from their seats and began to wander around. I sat there unsure of what to do. I began to panic silently.

"Nyomi." Isis walked up to us.

"Yeah?" I looked up at her.

"Two things. One, calm down and two, come with me." She pulled me from my seat.

"Isis." I groaned. "Where are you taking me?"

"Someone wants to say hi to you." She looked back at me.

"Great." I mumbled.

"Found her." She led us onto the platform where the superiors sat.

My heart began to race. Who was I meeting? Probably someone Isis wanted to hook me up with. I wasn't interested – I was just here to say that I came, not to make this a part of my life. I couldn't be like them and lie to my parents every week. And besides, they said no love connections outside of our dimension and I knew almost every boy in mine. They were all immature and reckless. My parents definitely wouldn't let me date someone of that nature, especially if they were from a lower class.

I noticed someone very familiar standing on the podium.

"Veronica?" I grabbed her hand.

"Hey." She said nervously. "You come here? Since when?"

"This is my first time." I answered shyly. "And yourself?"

"I'm a superior." She admitted.

"Okay, this is too weird." I chuckled. "Pretend this never happened?"

"Agreed." She nodded. "See you at home."

"Nyomi." Catarina stole me away and pulled me in for a hug.

"Hey Catarina." I hugged her tighter.

"Isis filled me in on the cover." She whispered in my ear.

I missed her so much. My only cousin was also one of my closest friends. I loved Catarina like she was my own sister. I'd been begging my parents to move her back in ever since they kicked her out my sophomore year over something as stupid as dating a boy from a different class. That night Shane proposed to her and she packed up her things and left Oxenfurt and me. I knew she was happy but I couldn't stand the fact that I wasn't a part of her life anymore.

I became so overwhelmed with emotions that my eyes watered.

"What's wrong?" She held me.

"I- I just miss you." I laughed it off.

"I miss you more." She kissed my forehead. "I can't believe you came here. Where do your parents think you are?"

"My house." Isis intervened.

"You lie now?" She looked down at me.

"It's new." I sniffled.

"Well everyone." She looked at her 11 friends sitting behind us. "This is my little cousin Nyomi."

They all smiled and waved and without making eye contact and I returned the gesture.

"So, who are you going to introduce yourself to?" She asked, returning to her seat.

"Do I really have to?" I groaned.

"Yes, I did the first part for you. They know your name, now just ask them theirs." She assured me.

"Fine." I sighed.

"You'll be fine." She insisted. "Come find me when you are done."

"Okay." I walked away nervously.

I knew who I wanted to meet.

I just was too nervous to remember the question that I had. I slowly walked over to the pale faces and swallowed hard.

"Hello." I approached a superior.

He was flawless as to be expected. His black hair complimented his skin complexion perfectly. He looked like he was in his mid- 20's, the body builder type. He was definitely someone Isis would be into and completely out of my league.

"Hi." He smiled at me.

I could feel small trembles throughout my body. My eyes were glued to him and only him. I knew that if I looked away I would only lose focus.

"My name Is Nyomi and yours?" I reached out to shake his hand.

"It's Rowan." He shook my hand.

"I think the question is what do you like to do?" I said unsure.

"I like to travel the dimensions." He winked.

"That's cool." I smiled.

"Yeah." He looked down at his phone.

"Well, see you around. Bye." I quickly walked away.

"You would choose the 3rd dimension." Isis smiled.

"So what are we doing?" I swallowed the lump in my throat.

"We're going to the 2nd floor." She led the way.

"When is this over?" I asked as we got in the elevator.

"Midnight." Catarina admired herself in the elevator mirror.

"And if they don't get out by midnight they'll be stuck in our dimension until the next night." Isis put on her lip gloss.

"That's a big risk." I simpered.

"Yeah, all of this is really." She shrugged.

The elevator doors opened up and the large room was filled with beings. The room was split in half. The front of the room was where the range was – it had 12 stations. The other half of the room was filled with bleachers. Every other station there were three small targets. I assumed those were for experienced archers and the single targets were for the amateurs.

"Wanna join?" Catarina asked as she browsed for a bow on the wall.

"No. I just like to look cute at these types of things." Isis flipped her hair and looked for a spot on the bleachers. "Coming X?"

"Actually, I want to." I smirked.

"What? Are you sure?" She grabbed my hand.

"Positive." I kissed her hand and joined Cat at the wall.

"Here, use this one." She handed me a gold bow and matching arrow that had the initials C.T.B engraved in them.

"CTB." I rubbed my thumb across the letters.

"Catarina Talia Briarwood." She said proudly. "Or Cynthia Tamara Briarwood, whichever."

"This was Aunt Cynthia's?" I looked up at her.

"Yes." She nodded. "Every Superior has one, she just passed hers down to me when she left the games. So I use hers."

"What? Here." I handed it back to her.

"I want you to use it." She refused.

"Too much pressure." I shook my head.

"You can do it though." She assured me as she grabbed a random bow and arrow off of the wall.

"Don't count on it." I frowned.

"You've done this before, Xena." She reminded me.

"Yeah, when I was younger." I shrugged.

"So you can do it now." She smiled.

"I – I." I stuttered.

"Please, for Mom." She whined.

"Fine." I gave in instantly.

"Perfect." She walked me over to the range.

"Who else is playing?" I looked around. "Anyone we know?"

"I don't know. You never really know until they show up." We walked over to station 6 and 7.

"Seriously?" I stared at the single target, feeling slightly offended.

"What?" She looked around.

"You know what." I rolled my eyes. "I can do better than this."

"Just do that one first." She insisted.

"Fine." I sighed.

The other stations filled quickly except for the one next to me.

"Ready?" She looked at me as she raised her bow.

"Yes." I smiled.

"Not to make fun but aren't you a little too short for those targets? " She said seriously.

"I'll be fine." I lied.

I was beyond nervous and standing at 5'2. I was easily the shortest person in the room and the targets were unusually high, but I was up for the challenge. I raised the bow and put the arrow in place. I quickly studied my target and the velocity.

A boy quickly appeared next to me. I tried not to stare but I couldn't help it. All I could see was the side of his face. But I could tell who he was – *what* he was. He was a pale face. His hair so perfect, not even a strand was out of place. His jawline was perfectly cut and his scent. His scent made my head spin.

"Go Nyomi!" Isis blurted from the stands.

I glanced over at the boy who was already looking at me. I shot him a quick smile and stopped myself. I needed to focus. Boys needed to be the furthest thing from my mind right now.

"Alright Archers, you ready?" A man shouted.

I positioned myself. I stared at the initials that were burning a hole in my soul at the moment. This meant more to me than to anyone here. This was for my aunt – in her memory. I knew I could easily take the shot. It was just the fact that she was gone and this bow was hers. She probably held it in her hands for the first time when she was my age and definitely Catarina's. She was part of the reason we could stand here today.

"Loose!" He demanded.

I effortlessly released my arrow and it went spiraling directly to the middle of the target. I stood back proudly.

"Nice." Cat whispered.

I could see the boy staring at me now. I hid my nervousness and continued to talk to Cat. She got pulled away by a friend, leaving the two of us standing side by side awkwardly. As soon as he approached me, I froze.

"That was impressive Miss-" His voice drifted off, waiting for my response.

"Nyomi." I blushed.

"Nyomi." He smiled.

"And your name?" I asked shyly.

"Blacksfer. Owen Blacksfer." He reached his hand out to shake mine.

"Nice to meet you." I met his reach and we locked eyes.

His eyes were so beautiful. They were hazel with a trim of gold. Definitely something I could get lost in.

"Pleasure is all mine." He smiled, my hand still in his.

"Nyomi!" Cat interrupted.

"Oh, I see you've met Owen." She glanced down at our hands smiling.

"Yeah, I have." I finally pulled my hand away.

"Cat." He smiled at her. "How are you today? Enjoying the games?"

"I'm great and you? Where's Rowan?" She hid her smile.

"I believe on the 3rd floor." He glanced at me and then back at Cat.

I stood there watching them converse for a minute. I watched his mouth move lightly and swiftly. I watch the perfection in his facial expressions. I was going to interrupt them until I saw Isis running towards me.

"Nyomi." She barged over.

"Hey Isis." I smiled.

"Nice shot!" She complimented me.

"Thanks." I nodded. "I'm going to do the next round."

"Oh no you're not. You're coming with me to the 3rd floor." She pulled me away before I could say anything.

"Isis." I looked back at Owen as she dragged me into the elevator.

"What?" She smiled breathlessly.

"Where's your hot guy?" I folded my arms.

"He's feeding, why?" She shrugged.

"Let's go find him so you start a conversation with him and then I can steal you away." I suggested sarcastically.

"Why would you do that?" She looked at me confused.

"Because you just did that to me!" I whined.

"Oh." She giggled. "I'm sorry X, I didn't know."

"It's fine, it's fine." I brushed it off.

"He was really hot though." She smiled.

"I know." I whined.

"What's his name?" She rubbed against me.

"Owen." I laughed.

"I like it." She nodded. "Owen."

"Keep your eyes on your dog." I smirked.

"You aren't even supposed to be into boys anyways." She teased.

"I'm not." I hissed. "I just think he is cute, that's all."

"Right." She drawled.

"Why are we back on the 1st floor?" I asked as the doors opened.

"Aren't you hungry?" She rubbed her stomach.

"What time is it?" I pulled my phone from my pocket.

I had 2 missed calls and 5 text messages from my parents. I stood there too petrified to open the notifications.

"Crap." I groaned. "We have to go outside really quick."

"Why? I'm hungry." She walked towards the table of food.

"This is why." I shoved my phone in her face.

"Let's go out the back." She nodded.

She pulled me through the crowd and through a sliding door that led into a kitchen area.

"Out here." She telepathically moved the bookcase and pulled me outside. "Call."

"Okay." I took a deep breath.

I dialed my Mother's number and waited for her to pick up.

"Xena Nyomi Briarwood!" She shouted.

"Yes Mother?" I bit my lip.

"Where are you?" She hissed.

"I'm with Isis." I spoke truthfully.

"Where?" I could hear her tapping her foot.

"Her mother took us out to eat and we're going to go see a movie." I lied.

Isis' eyes got big. I didn't mean to lie. I just couldn't stop once I started and I had no logical excuse for this.

"I need you home tonight. No excuses. We have important things to discuss." She revealed.

"But-" I whined.

"Tonight Xena." She demanded.

"The movie will be long though." I assured her.

"Oh really? How long exactly?" She huffed.

"Help." I mouthed to Isis.

"What's that mom? 1 AM?" She played along.

"Isis' mom said we won't be back until about 1. Is that okay? I can just come in the morning." I said nervously.

"1 am is fine. See you then." She hung up.

"What did she say?" Isis sighed.

"I have to be home at 1." I looked at her.

"Oh, That's plenty of time." She assured me.

"We have to go soon." I said nervously.

"Relax X. We can leave in an hour or so. It's only 9:30." She reminded me.

"Fine." I sighed.

"Hey." A whisper traveled from the darkness.

"Who's there?" Isis rolled her eyes.

"Close your eyes." He whispered back.

"Isis." I grabbed her hand.

"Shh." She ordered me. "It's okay."

A black figure lunged from the darkness and pushed her against the brick wall. I thought he was hurting her at first but they were just making out aggressively. I then realized that was her hot guy. I awkwardly walked back inside.

"Nyomi!" She shouted after me.

I walked through the lounge and sat down on the couch. I couldn't stop thinking of the reasons my mother wanted me home and how being here wasn't worth me getting caught.

"Hey beautiful." Dax walked up to me.

I knew Dax from my parents' meetings and parties. Even though he was a human, his father was a good friend of my parents. I also knew that Dax had the biggest crush on me since I was in middle school and he was a sophomore in high school.

"Hi." I faked a smile.

"So, I hear you're about to graduate, Lovebuggy." He sat down and wrapped his arm around me.

"Yeah." I giggled uncomfortably. "A couple more weeks."

"Wow." He gasped. "Weeks?"

"That's what my principal says." I shrugged from under his arm.

"Am I invited?" He played with a piece of my hair.

"I'm sure my parents will invite yours so, yeah." I looked down.

"Are you nervous?" He grabbed my chin, forcing me to look at him.

I could smell the beer on his breath.

"Are you drunk?" I broke free from his grip.

"If I say yes can I get a kiss?" He puckered his lips.

"If I say no, can you get a clue?" I pushed him away.

"What do you mean no? Don't you see how much money I have? Look at my cufflinks. Do you think this is cheap? Look at my shoes. Do you think I bought them off of a random vendor? Look at my watch. Do you see the diamonds? This one outfit can buy the lives of most of the attending middle class. I'm a very wealthy young man. I can make you an even richer young lady." He bragged.

"That's just it. Unlike you, my family and the rest of the beings in Oxenfurt, I don't care about the amount of money you have or the diamonds you can buy me. I care about what lies in your heart and your values. Your morals, and your strengths. Your mind power and your ability to love selflessly. You don't embody any of that. You're too self centered only looking to feed your ego." I quietly scolded him.

"Feelings aren't everything. You have to have stability, a name for yourself, some authority in life or else beings are going to walk all over you." He waved his finger in my face.

"Get over yourself." I laughed in his face.

"Where's the sweet girl that I see at dinners and at meetings with our families? The one that tucks her napkin in her shirt and places one on her lap even though she only takes one bite of food? Where's the girl that wouldn't say much of anything and let her parents speak for her? Where's the girl that's all about school and nothing else? The girl that wouldn't be caught here? The one that *cares* for her parents' image?" He slurred.

"She's gone!" I stormed off.

"What was that about?" Sarai stopped me. "That looked intense."

"I'm fine." I blinked the tears away.

"What happened?" She hugged me.

"Nothing." I shrugged.

"Something." She nagged. "Tell me now."

"Have you seen Cat?" I looked around.

"She's right there. She was just looking for you." She pointed. "Catarina!"

"You guys want to watch an archery competition?" Cat walked up to us.

"I don't know." I hesitated.

"I can't. I'm leaving early." Sarai complained.

"Why?" I pouted.

"Lisa and Lydia are my alibi and they are leaving." She shrugged.

"I love you. Call me tomorrow?" I hugged her.

"I will. Have fun." She hugged Cat and walked away.

"Come on Xena." Cat begged. "Owen will be there."

"He will?" I tried to hold back on my enthusiasm.

"Yes. Come on." She smiled as she pulled me away.

"What is up with everyone pulling me away? I can walk." I groaned.

"Anyone that knows you, knows that you have to be dragged somewhere." She looked back at me.

"2nd floor here we come!" She cheered.

"Hurry up, hurry up!" She pulled me in the elevator.

I got butterflies in my stomach and knots in my brain. I was so anxious. I wanted to see him but I wanted to go home. I wanted to get his number and I wanted to burn him from my memory. I knew that a boy like that would never be interested in a girl like me. Telling myself anything otherwise would be completely injudicious.

When we got inside, the room was completely dark and everyone was cheering. I couldn't see anything but Cat's hand in mine as she led me onto the bleachers. When we finally sat down, the show lights flickered on and there was Owen in the middle of the arena. There were two huge holographic tigers growling at him as he stood next to the superior I met earlier. They both had archer bags and crossbows in their hands with their backs facing the audience.

"Witches and Warlocks, Humans and Vamps, and uh, last but not least Werewolves." The host began. "Tonight's game is honoring a superior from the 3rd dimension Rowan and his little brother Owen. You all know the rules by now, and if you don't, well, just stay off my floor and remain the hell behind the fence."

"Brothers?" I grinned.

"Hot huh?" She nudged me.

Somehow I made eye contact with Owen – probably because I was staring at him already. He smirked at me and turned back around. I felt someone a row above me put their hands over my eyes. I quickly removed them and turned around fearful that it was Dax, thankfully it was Zoe.

"Oh, hey." I sighed in relief.

"Hi." She smirked.

"It's time!" The host yelled. "You have 60 seconds to prepare."

I leaned back onto Zoe's legs and got comfortable.

"He's kinda cute." She leaned over me and pointed to Owen.

"Back off Zoe, that's Xena's Boo." Cat teased.

"I'm-"

"She's gay." I mocked her.

"But your boo since when?" Zoe congratulated me.

"He's not my boo. I don't even know him." I whispered.

"Yet." Cat interjected.

"What would Mommy and Daddy think?" Zoe teased me.

"They will think nothing of it because it isn't happening-"

"Yeah, yeah." She shoved a candy stick in my mouth.

No matter what she fed me to stop me from talking it wasn't happening. My parents would die if they knew I was friends with someone from another dimension let alone dating one. He was cute and seemed nice but I wasn't going to ruin my parents' reputation over him.

As Owen and his brother charged at the tigers, my phone began to vibrate in my pocket. I quickly pulled it out and it was Isis. I answered and plugged one ear.

"Hello?" I whispered.

"You and Sarai meet me at the car, now." She sounded frantic.

"Sarai left. Why what's wrong?" I leaned forward.

"My parents got back early. We have to go." She sniffled.

"Do they know where we are?" I stood up at the same time as the crowd began to cheer for Owen.

"Not exactly. I panicked and told them we were at your house." She admitted.

"And you say *I* can't lie?" I hissed as I headed down the bleachers.

"Where are you going?" Cat whined.

"Home." I frowned.

"I need a ride." Zoe grabbed my hand.

"Zoe's coming." I pulled her down the stairs and out of the door.

When we got to the car, Isis already had the engine running. I could see the fear in her eyes as we climbed in the car. We rode in silence all the way home.

"You stick to your story and I'll stick to mine." Isis said as we pulled at home.

"Okay. WT later?" I hugged her.

"Of course." She promised.

"I'm spending the night with who exactly?" Zoe leaned on the middle console.

"Me." Isis looked back at her.

"Don't worry. It'll be okay Xena." Isis assured me.

"Bye guys." I got out of the car.

"We love you." They both whispered as they pulled off.

I braced myself and walked up the steps to my house.

They could tell me anything at this point. I needed to put on the biggest show and prepare to lie about every single detail about tonight.

I put my key in and slowly unlocked the door.

"Xena, is that you?" My mother snatched the door open.

"Yes Mother, it's me." I faked a smile.

"What are you wearing?" She frowned.

My heart dropped to the floor. I forgot to change on the way home.

"Well." She crossed her arms.

"We were playing dress up. It was just for fun." I assured her. "You know I don't dress like this."

"Join me in your father's office now." She disappeared.

I closed the front door and placed my keys on the rack.

A lump formed in my throat as I slowly walked in the office. She was sitting at his desk with 5 envelopes in her hand.

"What's that?" I stood by the door.

"Come sit down." She looked at the chair.

"Okay." I slowly walked across the room.

"Xena." She said anxiously.

"What's this ab-"

"Open them." She tossed the letters in front of me as I sat down.

They were letters from colleges. Either they were acceptances or rejections. I knew that and that didn't scare me at all. I wasn't looking forward to college, not anymore. It was what my parents wanted for me, as always. I grabbed the envelopes and ripped them open. All five of them held gold papers inside. I knew what that meant. I sat them back down on the desk.

"You got into all of them!" My mother exclaimed.

"Oh wow." I faked a smile.

"I'm so proud of you!" She shrieked. "And your father will be too!"

"I know." I nodded.

"Why don't you seem excited about this Xena?" She sighed.

"I am excited." I lied. "Nothing makes me happier. I'm just tired."

"Well, that's all. You can go back over to Isis' if you'd like." She said sincerely.

"Actually, I'm just going to turn in for the night." I pretended to stretch.

"Okay sweetie, I'll see you in the morning." She smiled down at the letters.

"Okay." I stood up and headed to the door.

"Oh, one more thing." She stopped me.

"Yes Mother?" I turned to face her.

"Burn those clothes when you get a chance." She smiled.

"Of course." I nodded. "Night."

I ran upstairs to my room and locked my door. As soon as I collapsed on my bed, my tears couldn't wait to spill over onto my clean sheets. I knew that colleges would want me but I was hoping that they didn't. I was hoping that they would just reject me or at least waitlist me. I didn't want to go to college. I just wanted to be myself. Maybe become a writer or a photographer. Something that made *me* happy. Getting a degree in divine witchcraft wasn't going to make me happy, I'd be miserable. I'd be doing something that I didn't want to do for beings that only cared for themselves. I was tired of living for my parents. I was tired of dressing like I worked for the president when I was just a normal teenage girl. I wanted to find myself but my parents were trying their hardest to make me lose sight of who I wanted to be. I started to cry harder as I gave into my emotions. I cried so much that the tears stopped and just silent sobs continued. Helpless, hopeless sobs.

III: CONTEMPTIBLE

"Xena, wake up." Veronica lightly shook me awake.

"What? What time is it?" I opened my sore eyes.

"It's 4:30." She chuckled.

"In the morning?" I pulled my blanket over my head. "Why am I being woken up exactly?"

"We have to start the preparation of the festival for Monday-"

"Do you hear yourself?" I whined. "For Monday. It's Saturday."

"Your fathers' wishes." She sighed. "You can call over your friends."

"I don't care." I turned away from her.

"I made your favorite meal from the 1st dimension!" She sang.

"Bacon and cheese stuffed croissants?" I peeked from under the blanket.

"Go shower." She walked out.

In my shower I thought about Owen even though I didn't want to. I thought about his eyes, his smile, his scent – I could never forget. I wanted to relive that night over and over. It was better than I thought it would be. Actual fun. My friends were right and I had no regrets. I wanted to go again. I wanted to see Owen again.

I stepped out of the shower into my silky robe. When I walked into my room, Isis was lying on my bed with her face resting in her palms.

"Hey." She smiled.

"Hi." I smiled back.

"So, how was it last night?" She rolled off the bed and walked towards me.

"It was fun." I admitted.

"I meant with your mom." She smirked.

"Oh." I giggled. "It was pointless. She wanted me to open college applications to see if I got in, just to tell me I could go back to your house."

"Wow." She raised her eyebrow. "She's such a control freak."

"Who's a control freak?" My mother walked in.

"Can you knock, Mother?" I tried to cover my exposed body parts.

"Just bringing your attire for Monday." She waved the cleaners bag.

"Thank you Mother." I nodded.

"Also, we're having a family dinner tonight." She added.

"With who?" I asked skeptically.

"Isis will be there." She closed the door behind herself.

"I wonder why." Isis frowned. "Do you think we're in trouble?"

"Wait." I tiptoed to my door and pressed my ear against it.

I waited until I heard my mother's voice downstairs.

"What were you saying?" I looked back at Isis.

She pulled a black bag from her purse. "Do it with me this time."

"We have a family dinner tonight about God knows what. No way!" I shook my head.

"Just one time. Sarai and the girls are on the way. They're doing it too." She tried to persuade me.

"I'm sorry, but no. I need a clear mind for tonight." I walked into my closet.

"Fine." She sighed dramatically. "I won't ask anymore."

"Thank you." I rolled my eyes.
"Ever again." She sighed again.

"Okay." I walked back into my room ignoring her obvious hints.

I knew what she was doing. She was trying to guilt trip me but it wasn't going to work. I wasn't going to risk doing drugs and getting caught. My plans on leaving for my 18th birthday would be ruined and I couldn't jeopardize that. I needed to get out of here. Out of this town.

"Every teenager does this." She protested.

"Not this one." I pulled my hair into a french braid.

"X?" Sarai knocked at my door.

"It's open!" I shouted.

Sarai, Zoe, and Lydia walked in with big grins on their faces.

"So, where is it?" Sarai rushed over to Isis.

"Right here." Isis dangled the bag in her face.

"Let me see." Lydia snatched it.

"I wanna see too!" Zoe peeked over her shoulder.

"Let's do it now!" Sarai reached to lock my door.

"Uh. I can't have my door locked." I reminded her.

"So, you couldn't talk her into it." She stared at Isis.

"Do you know how hard that is?" Isis scoffed.

"You had one job." Zoe laughed.

"Technically I scored the drugs, that's two jobs." Isis pointed out. "One out of two isn't bad."

"True." Lydia smiled.

"Everyone in a circle." Isis ordered as she sat down on the ground.

"Wait, you're going to do it in here?" I asked nervously.

"Where else would we go?" Sarai looked up at me.

"You need to relax." Zoe pulled me into the circle.

"I'm fine." I sat down and wrapped my arms around my legs.

"You're not fine." Sarai shook her head. "You're the opposite of fine."

"Sometimes I wish I could charm you into relaxation." Isis groaned.

Everyone looked at Isis and then at me smiling.

"Good thing that's against the rules." I smirked nervously.

"I don't mind breaking a rule or two." Isis grabbed her wand. "What about you girls?"

"Nope." Zoe smiled.

"Not at all." Sarai chimed in.

"Tell them Lyd." I pleaded.

"It's for your own good, X." Lydia nodded.

"Not you too." I groaned. "Great, now all of my friends are against me."

"Only because we want what's best for you." Isis promised.

"This is what normal teenagers do. Smoke a little, drink a little, lose our virginity on prom night, graduate and become more serious. Right now is our time to party and let loose. Get caught and break hearts. Senior year is our year. I've been friends with you all since I moved here in 3rd grade. I trust you girls with my life. So please, don't make our last year being together so boring." Zoe preached.

"Okay, you've been watching way too many movies from the 1st dimension." I chuckled.

"Yeah, Zoe is right." Sarai stood to her feet. "Besides college is where the fun really starts."

"Sucks we won't all be together." Lydia frowned.

"But we'll still have each other." Isis smiled.

"I love you guys." Lydia sniffled.

I stared at everyone wallowing and I knew I felt the same way. I've known these girls my entire life. How could I just up and leave them in a few months?

"I love you guys too." I hugged them.

We stood in a huddle for a moment. It felt good to know they were as sad as I was.

"I'll do it." I pulled away.

"What?" Isis grinned.

"I said I'll do it." I repeated myself.

"Don't feel pressured." Lydia placed her hand on my shoulder.

"I don't. I'm tired of living in my parents' shadow. Doing what they want me to do. Afraid to do what I want to do. I'm over it." I grabbed the bag from Sarai.

"What are you doing?" Isis rushed to my side.

"I just have to eat them right?" I stared down at the brownies in the bag.

"Yes. Not even the whole thing. Just a few bites." She instructed.

"There's one for each of us." She reached her hand in the bag.

She placed a brownie in each of our hands.

"Ready?" Isis raised the brownie to her mouth.

"Yes." I nodded.

"Girls!" My mother barged in and we dropped our hands awkwardly.

"Give me those." She put her hand out. "You'll ruin your appetite."

"But Mother." I hesitated.

"But nothing." She reached for my brownie. "It's way too early."

We all placed our brownies in her hand shamefully.

"You all can have these back after breakfast." She walked out leaving the door open. "Let's go."

"What do we do?" I panicked.

"We're screwed." Zoe shook her head in disbelief.

"Not exactly." Isis smiled. "All we have to do is say we aren't hungry."

"You make it sound so easy." I hissed.

"It will be." She assured me.

"Xena!" My mother shouted after us.

"Coming Mother." I rushed out of the room.

We peeked around the corner, and into the kitchen. My father was standing at the island washing his hands and Mother was at the stove.

"Whose are these?" He stared down at the brownies on the counter.

"Xena's." My mother plated our food.

"Well, I'm stealing one." He picked one up and put it to his lips.

My heart began to pound out of my chest. If he were to even take a bite, my life would be over. Right when I was about to intervene, my mother pulled the brownie from his mouth.

"You'll spoil your breakfast." She warned.

"Where is that girl?" She mumbled to herself. "Xena!"

Isis pushed me into their view.

"There you are." My mother stared at me.

"Here I am." I nodded.

"What's wrong with you? Why do you seem so off this morning?" She handed me my plate.

I said nothing. Silence was better than a lie that I didn't want to tell.

"I know what it is." My mom smirked. "You want those brownies."

"Veronica." My mother called her name as soon as she walked in.

"Yes?" She forced a smile.

"Can you saran-wrap these for Xena?" She handed her the plate.

"Sure thing." Veronica nodded.

"There. Out of sight, out of mind." My mother smiled as she cut my food into little pieces.

"I'm just not hungry." I lied.

"Xena." My father said seriously as he sat down across from my mother. "Breakfast is the most important meal and you know that. Veronica made breakfast. So everyone is eating. Now go get your friends."

"Yes, sir." I nodded before going to find them.

"We heard him." Isis groaned as she walked past me.

"Yeah, nice try X." Sarai rubbed my shoulder.

"Good morning Girls." My father flashed a fake smile at them.

"Good morning." They all answered as they took their seats.

"So, today we will be setting up the front yard." He started. "Then we will work our way to the backyard."

"Xena knows we will be working hard today. That is why all of her friends are here to help." My mother chimed in.

"So girls, Did Xena tell you all that she got accepted to five colleges including my Alma Mater?" My father bragged.

"Really?" Sarai smiled. "That's great!"

"Isn't it?" My mother smirked.

"It is." Lydia added.

"What about you girls?" My father asked, cleaning his plate.

"Well, I'm going to Palos University." Isis smirked.

"Excellent." My father smirked back.

"I'm going to go to the community for two years and then I'm going to Veles." Lydia added.

"Nice plan." He nodded.

"I honestly don't have a plan." Zoe shrugged. "I want to go to school but my father insists that I stay focused on my magic."

"Your father is a-" He stopped himself. "You can only get so far with magic."

"I know." She nodded.

"Okay, we're done eating." I forced down the last undesired bite.

"What's the rush?" My mother sipped her coffee.

"Just anxious to start setting up!" I lied through my teeth.

"That's my girl." My father stood up.

"Let's go to the front. Everything is already out there." He led us.

"Veronica." My mother stopped her.

"Yes?" She answered.

"Don't forget to do the dishes before you join us." She reminded her before she walked out.

Everyone continued on as I watched Veronica collect the plates.

She looked so sad, so unfulfilled. Always doing what she was told, never doing anything for herself. I could tell she was tired of this life and I could relate.

I walked outside and joined everyone on the front steps.

There were unassembled platforms and banners everywhere. It was like the presidential inauguration for the human dimension. It was the most color I've seen in our town in a very long time. We spent all day decorating the house from the front to the back. The day passed so much quicker than I thought it would. Everyone ended up leaving besides Isis and Zoe. My parents left soon after the crowd. They said something about a practice press conference. I was just glad that I had my speech planned out for the last six months so I didn't have to go with them.

"So now what?" Isis asked as we climbed the stairs to my room.

"First, I'm going to shower and get ready for the family dinner." I simpered.

"And then?" She drawled.

"And then, you two are going to steal back those brownies." I pulled my robe from its hook.

"Family dinner?" Zoe asked confused.

"Yeah, you're welcome to stay." I smiled at her.

"What time is it?" She glanced at her wristwatch. "Actually, I better get going. I have to babysit tonight."

"Can we trade places?" I whined.

"And be here with your strict ass parents? No thank you." She pulled her bag from my vanity chair.

"Fine." I pouted. "Call me when you get home?"

"I will." She nodded. "Walk me out Isis?"

"Of course." Isis grabbed her hand. "I'll be back."

I glanced up at my wall clock. It was 7:30 and dinner started at 8. I rushed into the shower frantically.

"What time is it?" I flung the bathroom door open.

"7:45 why?" Isis sat up.

"Dinner starts at 8." I groaned.

"Why are you freaking out? It's just dinner." She shrugged.

"Just dinner? Have you met my parents?" I chuckled dryly.

"Yeah. I thought my parents were strict until I saw the full extent of yours." She chided. "How are you ever going to have a boyfriend?"

"I won't. My father says I can't have a boyfriend until I'm married." I unraveled my hair and let the loose curls fall down my back.

"Does that even make sense?" She smirked.

"In his world it does." I sighed as I slipped on my camisole.

"Xena!" My father shouted from downstairs.

I sighed before rushing to the door. "Yes father?"

"Dinner!" He replied.

"Come on." I looked in the mirror one last time before leaving.

Everything and everyone had to be perfect for dinner. Even if it was just for family.

"Good evening." Veronica greeted us as we reached the bottom of the stairs.

"Good evening." I nodded, smiling.

"Your father has guests." She whispered.

"I know, it's Isis and her family." I assured her as we walked by.

"Xena, wait!" She called after me.

"Yes?" I smiled back at her.

"It's Dax." She bit her lip.

"Dax?" I dropped Isis' hand.

"He's here?" Isis intervened.

"He and his family are already at the dinner table." She nodded.

"Great." I groaned. "Thanks for the heads up, V."

What could be the reason for Dax being here? Was it because of the meeting or me? Either way I didn't want him here. We walked in and everyone stopped their conversations and stared at us.

"Hello Xena." My godparents greeted me.

"Hello." I smiled at them.

"What are you guys doing here?" I looked at Dax and his family.

"They are staying in our guest house until Monday night after the press conference meeting." My father spoke for them.

"Oh." I faked a smile.

"Join us." Dax stood to his feet to give me his seat.

I wasn't going to move a muscle until my parents instructed me to.

"Are your feet glued to the floor?" Isis hissed in my ear before she walked over and took her seat next to her family.

"Xena." My father cleared his throat. "Don't be rude. Dax is trying to give you his seat."

"I don't want his seat." I muttered.

"Xena." My parents scoffed.

"It's fine." Dax smiled at them. "I should be used to this behavior by now."

"What behavior are you referring to exactly?" My mother asked curiously.

He wouldn't.

"Well, the other night Xena and I were talking and she was kind of in this funk." He started.

"Oh, where were you guys? I don't remember seeing you at the house." My mother looked at me.

"Where were we again, Xena?" He smirked.

"Fine." I walked over to the table and plopped down.

"What were you saying Dax?" My father smiled at him.

"I popped up at her school on Friday." He winked at me.

"She's been very stressed and on edge lately." My mother nodded. "It's because of her valedictorian speech, college essays, competition, and her speech for Monday."

"That does sound stressful." Dax's mother added.

"It is." I stared down at my plate.

"So Xena, we were thinking that you and Dax-" My father started.

"Should what?" I tried to hold my composure.

"We think it's best for both the 1st and the 4th dimension, if you both consider being together. You would be the most powerful couple. As far as wealth and authority goes. You would take over this dimension when your mother and I step down and Dax would do the same for his parents. It's what's best for everyone." He explained proudly.

"For everyone?" I huffed. "Everyone but me."

"I'm all for it." Dax interrupted. "I just don't think Xena is into me in *that* way."

"You're right, I'm not." I chuckled as I played with my food. "I'm not marrying Dax."

"Whoa, whoa, whoa, Slow down. No one said anything about marriage." My father retorted. "Just a relationship, even a close friendship. As long as you reproduce and you appear as a couple you should be fine."

"Mother?" I looked at her with tears in my eyes.

"I stand with your father on this one." She said confidently.

I couldn't believe this was happening.

My parents were arranging my marriage without my consent. They were willing to give me away to a boy who didn't even know me to love me. How could everyone at this table be in agreement with something so sinister. I stared over at Isis whose eyes were already on me.

"Godparents?" I stared at her parents hopefully.

"We agree with the friendship part or at least pretending, my love." Isis' father answered.

"I – I can't believe this." I pushed my chair from the table.

"Xena, don't." My mother ordered. "Just listen to what they have to say."

"Unbelievable." I stood to my feet. "I'm going to my room."

"If you walk away from this table do not come back downstairs for the rest of the night!" My father bellowed.

"Fine!" I stormed off.

"Xena, wait!" Isis chased after me.

"For what? For my own parents to sell me to the highest bidder?" I bawled.

"I know, I'm sorry." She hugged me.

"Why would they do this to me?" I broke down in her arms. "Don't they love me?"

"Yes." She shushed me. "Of course they do. They are just so blinded by their image that they aren't paying attention to the expense of it all."

"What do I do?" I sniffled.

"Let's go to your room. I have an idea." She pulled me up the stairs and down the hallway.

"What are you doing?" I tried to break free of her grip.

"Come on." She closed my door behind us.

"Lock it." I ordered.

"But I thought you said-"

"I know what I said. What are we doing?" I sat down on my bed.

"This." She reached into my top drawer and pulled out the brownies. "Do you think you can handle it?"

"Give me one." I nodded as I wiped the rest of my tears away.

She placed the brownie in my hand and walked into the bathroom.

I shoved the brownie in my mouth and chewed it really fast. It tasted like a mixture of chocolate and dirt. I sat there struggling to swallow it when she walked back in.

"Where'd the brownie go?" She smiled at me.

"I – I ate it." I smiled back.

"The whole thing? It was for us to share." She rushed over to me. "I told you that we were supposed to only eat a few bites."

"Why? What's going to happen to happen to me?" I asked frantically.

"You're about to have the best trip of your life." She grinned.

"The best?" I smirked.

She explained what the brownies were made of and I didn't understand a thing. I just knew they were something similar to the drugs they ate in the human dimension but way stronger because they were made by witches.

The next day, I didn't leave my room. I didn't care if I was hungry or if I was thirsty. I ate another brownie and forced myself to sleep. I didn't want to see my parents' faces anymore. I didn't want to feel the shame I felt when they told me. I just didn't want to feel anything.

IV: ASSEMBLAGE

"Go and get her out of her room now!" My father shouted. "The meeting is about the start and she isn't even up yet!"

"I'm going." My mother answered.

"Xena!" She slammed my door open.

I didn't react. I just sat there silently.

"You have 10 seconds to get dressed and get downstairs!" She hissed. "Today isn't the day to test my seriousness, Xena. I am at my wits end right now. I could literally rip my hair out and believe me I would but it's already falling out."

"Falling out? Really?" I hid my smirk.

"You know this means a lot to your father. Why would you intentionally sabotage the one day out of the year that he genuinely smiles?" She sighed.

"You are trying to sell me!" I cried.

"It was just a thought. No one said anything was set in stone. Look at it as a bad prank and now it's over." She insisted.

"So no more talk of this marriage?" I relaxed my posture.

"Not another word. Now please, get dressed." She walked out.

Knowing that my mother referred back to it as a bad prank made me feel better. It wasn't anything they were serious about, they were just exploring all options. It still made me cringe but I could shelf the betrayal for now.

I unzipped the garment bag on my bed and inside was a gray blazer with gold buttons wrapped around a white camisole. The blazer had two front pockets that were trailed with black along gray slacks to match. The black and white wallet with three gold studs on the latch was absolutely stunning. It had to have just been ordered from the human dimension because I had never seen it before. There was a black watch for one wrist and gold bangles for the other. Of course at the bottom of the bag were black high heels from hell. They added at least 3 inches to my height.

I slipped my clothes on and sat down at my vanity. I stared up at the cue cards taped to my mirror for my speech of appreciation. I placed my hair in a tight bun on top of my head as my dress code permits. I grabbed my makeup bag and lightly tickled my cheeks with the pink powder. I put on my mascara and stood to my feet. I grabbed my retainer from my vanity and put it in. The retainer was fake. It was to add the *perfect* image. Innocent girl that doesn't show any appealing body parts, that connects intellectually and not psychically. It was time to put my acting to work.

I looked at myself in the mirror one last time before walking out of my room. I peeked down the stairs and my house was full of beings as I expected. Butlers with wine glasses and appetizers. Why did I think it would be different? As I reached the bottom of the stairs everyone started greeting me warmly. I faked many smiles to get into the kitchen where I needed to be.

"Mother." I approached her and a crowd of tall women.

"Hello Xena." She smiled. "Glad you could make it."

"Glad to be here." I smiled back.

"Let's join your father in the backyard. He is about to give his speech." She sipped her wine and led the way.

As we stepped into the backyard, I saw my father standing at the podium preparing for his speech. I stared at the many beings standing with their program in their hands, others were sitting patiently.

"Hello." My father started.

"First, I would like to call my family up to the stage. These two seats are reserved for my princess and queen, Azura and Xena." He clapped after announcing. "Come on up here."

My mother wrapped her arm around mine and gently pulled me down the pathway upon the podium. We sat down and stared at the crowd smiling. There was well over 5,000 being but I was used to it. I waited for my father to start up again.

"Now that they are present, I want to start by saying thank you for joining us for this dimensional appreciation meeting. It really means a lot to us that you are all here. Those of you from different dimensions, but are good friends of mine, Thank you for your support. And thank you Oxenfurt for loving your dimension the way you should." He said with a smile.

"Now, for important news, I need you all to understand the seriousness of the murders happening in all dimensions. We aren't sure who is taking these precious lives but I, Brice Briarwood, vow to find out and have them banished. I myself, lost a dear friend to the B.S.D also known as the Blue Snake Death." He lied.

He was nothing but a phony but I loved him regardless.

"Trust that your superiors will handle this." He promised. "*I* will handle this."

"You're up." My mother whispered to me.

"And now for my Daughter, Xena. She will be announcing the award winners and giving an appreciation speech." He reached for me as the crowd went wild.

"Knock 'em dead." He hugged me.

What a cynical choice of words.

I stepped onto the podium and stared past the crowd nervously. I knew what everyone expected me to say but I also knew what was burning inside me to expose. I stood there torn for a few seconds.

"It seems everyone I talk to wants me to express appreciation to this foundation, to the founders." I looked back at my father. "To this man, my father, your years of research and depth of understanding goes beyond what anyone else has done. Your ability to present in such an interesting way produced one of the most memorable evenings in our dimension's history. I personally appreciate your approach to anticipate other beings' intentions. The subject of our history intrigues me and I plan to learn more and more every day. These meetings are more than just an annual thing; they are our legacy. So without further ado, I will present the appreciation awards to the following." I smiled.

"Brice Briarwood, John St. Nolend, Edmond Whittingham, Samuel Chambers, Michael Leon, Jeffrey Rising, and Aldrin Blacksfer." I applauded them.

Blacksfer. Why did that name sound so familiar?

Next was the speeches.

The long, insincere, and rehearsed speeches. Thankfully, I was done for the most part. I stepped down from the podium and the crowd roared with satisfaction.

Isis' father took my place and grabbed a trophy from the table next to him.

"Thank you my beloved dimension." He started.

I watched as Isis walked down the aisle and took a seat in the front row. My father caught my attention with his painful stare. That look only meant one thing, I did something wrong. I casually walked over to where he was standing.

"Father." I smiled at him.

"Do you see your shirt?" He looked at me with a disgusted look on his face.

"What?" I looked down to see my camisole pulled too far down exposing the start to my cleavage.

"Fix yourself." He stormed away angrily.

"Don't you dare cry." Sarai rushed to my side.

"I always mess up somehow." My eyes watered.

"No one even noticed but him." She assured me.

"That's all that matters." I hissed.

"Well, Cat needs to see you." She linked her arm with mine as we walked away from the crowd.

"Where is she?" I looked around.

"I don't know. She isn't supposed to be here though. She's coming to tell you something. Just be on the lookout." She warned before walking away.

Why would Catarina sneak into my town when she knew she was banned? What could be so important that she had to see me today out of all days? I knew if she wasn't trying to be seen then she wouldn't be. I just had to wait for her to approach me, whenever that was.

I walked over to the refreshment table and grabbed a plate of delectable meats and fruits.

"Xena." Veronica appeared next to me with a plate.

"Hey V." I smiled at her.

"Your speech was perfect." She congratulated me.

"Tell that to my father." I hissed.

"I will." She looked around. "Found him. Let's go."

"Wait, why do I have to go?" I whined.

"Because he has a really cute guy with him. Maybe he will introduce you guys." She said excitedly as she pulled me in their direction.

"What? No. I don't want to talk to anyone." I tried to pull away.

"Just come on. I've met him a few times at the games. He's really cool." She tried to sell me.

"That's good for him." I stopped walking.

"Why are you so insecure?" She sighed.

"Because what would we talk about? This meeting? How proud I am of our dimension? I don't even want to be here." I crossed my arms.

"Fix your posture." She whispered. "Beings are starting to stare."

"I'm sorry." I relaxed my arms.

"Just be-" She trailed off. "What was your name for the games?"

"Nyomi?" I asked as if I didn't remember. Of course I did.

"Yes. Be Nyomi." She smiled.

"I thought we couldn't hook up with beings from different dimensions." I said sarcastically.

"You can't." She shrugged.

"Exactly my point." I turned to walk away then stopped.

She was right. I needed to stop running from things that challenged me and it wasn't like I knew the guy. He was probably just a part of another one of the snot-nosed dimensional separation tactics. My father pretended to care about everyone but he truly didn't have any regard for the beings he deemed below us. So whoever he was talking to had to be important. I could either ruin this for him or make him look good. Knowing that I had that option made me feel powerful.

"Hello?" Veronica interrupted my thoughts. "Are you even listening to me?"

"Fix your posture. Beings are starting to stare." I walked away.

"Where are you-" She stopped when she saw where I was headed.

I walked across the yard and a little past my father. I had a plan.

"Xena." He stopped me as I hoped he would.

"Yes Father?" I turned around slowly.

"Come meet my friends." He stopped the waiter.

"Gold star!" He placed his wine glass in my hand and grabbed one for himself.

Gold star meant they were either potential business partners or preexisting sponsors.

"Father." I looked down at the wine glass.

"Oh, just this one time Xena." He shrugged. "Here take this one too."

"Two drinks?" I looked up at him confused.

"Of course not. It's for our guests." He picked up another glass. "Let's go."

He held his arm out for me and I hesitantly linked arms with him.

As we walked over, I stared down at my feet. I didn't look up until I saw two sets of designer shoes a few feet from mine. I nervously looked up to meet my company.

"Gentlemen, This is my daughter Xena." My father introduced me. "Xena, this is Owen and Aldrin. They are from the 3rd dimension."

"Hello Xena." Owen smirked at me.

"Hello." I smirked back.

Owen? Why was he here? He knew my father? He was our gold star guest?

"Xena, that was an amazing speech you gave." Aldrin complimented me.

"Thank you." I nodded. "Congratulations on your award."

"Thank you." He smiled at me. "Such a polite daughter you have."

"Thank you." My father grinned at me. "She's the best."

"For you." My father handed Aldrin his other glass.

"Thank you. I was thinking about walking over to the refreshment table." He smiled happily.

"No problem." My father sipped his glass.

"Xena." My father looked down at my hands.

"Oh, right." I smiled bashfully as I handed Owen his glass.

His finger lightly brushed against mine as he took it.

"Dad?" A girl walked over to Aldrin.

"Yes dear?" He smiled at her.

"Jenny said her dad's inside, didn't you need to speak with him?" She asked.

"Phil? Yes I was just speaking with Brice about him." He nodded.

"Let's go talk to him about the investment we were discussing." My father suggested.

My heart began to race. Were we about to get left alone?

"Shall we?" My father led Aldrin into the house.

I felt my cheeks run hot as Owen smiled over at me. I smiled back as the butterflies filled my stomach. His perfectly chiseled face sent a chill down my spine. I'd never felt this way about anyone before. What was it about him?

"So, I'm going to take a wild guess and say your middle name is Nyomi?" He smiled.

"Guilty." I nodded.

"Walk with me?" He asked.

We walked further away from the crowd and over to our huge white fountain.

"Why did you leave the games so early? Too scared to get caught?" He smirked.

"Maybe." I hid my smile.

"Thanks for the glass." He nodded. "I can't decide which one I like better."

"What?" I sipped my drink.

"Nyomi or Xena." He pondered. "Which one do you like better?"

"Nyomi." I sat on the edge of the fountain.

"Xena." He disagreed.

"Why Xena?" I questioned him.

"Because it's who you really are." He sat down next to me.

"How do you know who I really am?" I stared at his mouth.

"Will I see you at the games?" He ignored my question.

"Yes." I nodded.

"Good because I'm going to beat you this time." He stepped onto the edge of the fountain.

"Owen." I looked up at him. "What are you doing?"

"Join me." He reached his hand out.

I looked around for my father and he was nowhere in sight. I didn't want to get caught being childish as my father would call it.

"Only for a second." I grabbed his hand and he pulled me up effortlessly into his arms.

"Oops." He stared down at his shirt ruined by my champagne.

"I am so sorry." I frowned.

"It's okay." He chuckled.

"Let me clean it for you." I stepped down off the ledge. "Please."

"Okay. I'll follow you." He motioned me to lead the way.

"Here." I tossed him the shirt I stole from my father's dresser.

"Your dads?" He stood to his feet.

"Yes." I nodded.

"Nice." He slowly unbuttoned his shirt and exposed his perfect body.

I couldn't help but stare at him. He was breathtaking. It was as if someone hand carved him to perfection. I couldn't help but blush.

"Come with me. I'll clean your shirt." I led him into my bathroom.

I placed his dirty clothes in the sink and grabbed my purple squirt bottle from underneath it. When I stood up he was in the mirror behind me.

"Have a seat." I smirked at him.

"Yes ma'am." He smirked back as he sat down on the toilet.

I sprayed my serum on his stain and waited for it to work its magic. Literally.

"What is that?" He watched me.

"It's my family's secret serum. It gets rid of stains almost instantly." I bragged as I sat on my counter.

I stared out the door to stop myself from staring at him. His smile, his smell.

Something about him made me not care about the rules and that was the opposite of what I needed. I needed to stay focused. I needed to keep a clear mind. I didn't need to be distracted by boys with model bodies and even better personalities. I needed to focus on school and my powers. That's what mattered the most, *right?*

"Is this a witch thing?" He grinned.

"Yes." I nodded. "It's been passed down through many generations."

"Intriguing. All that's passed down in my family are fangs." He joked.

"Fangs sound cooler than an old remedy for stains." I opined.

"They are not as cool as they seem." He demurred.

"Neither is this remedy. Your clothes will take some time." I warned him.

"Then I guess it's good you got me this." He waved the shirt around in the air. "Besides, I was hoping it wasn't an instant remedy."

He stepped in front of me and slipped his shirt on. I stared at him as his abs disappeared under the shirt. I quickly looked away before he saw me.

"Well, I can't go down there in your father's shirt." He laughed. "Will it be a problem if we stay in your room?"

Yes. Of course it would be.

"Of course not." I lied as we walked into my room.

He climbed in my bed and made himself comfortable, which I didn't mind.

"Is your dad always so serious?" He asked casually.

"Always." I sat down on the edge of the bed nervously.

I don't know why I was so nervous but the feeling I felt when I first saw him still hasn't faded. Same lump in my throat, same butterflies in my stomach.

He mumbled something I couldn't understand.

"What?" I asked, hoping he would repeat himself.

"Nothing. My father is the same way." He sighed.

"Picture perfect isn't always so perfect." I muttered.

"That should be my life's caption." He smirked.

"Yours?" I chuckled sourly.

"Ours then?" He chuckled back.

"Deal." I smirked looking down at my feet.

"Do you have any siblings?" He asked curiously.

"It's just me." I simpered.

"That's gotta suck." He frowned.

"Trust me, it does." I slipped my shoes off. "That girl was your-"

"Biggest headache, my little sister Charlotte." He smiled.

"And then there's Rowan, your brother." I added.

"Right. You met Rowan at the games." He nodded.

"My best friend Isis thinks he's gorgeous." I smirked.

I knew that the information would probably get back to him and Isis would be thanking me later. Although Isis had someone, she never settled down with anyone. She liked being spontaneous and was too much of a free spirit to ever be tied down.

"Do you think he's gorgeous?" He sat up.

"Not my type." I answered.

I knew that was the answer he wanted to hear and the one I truly meant. I didn't see him in any other way than an authority figure. It was Owen who I thought was breathtaking but I would never openly admit that.

"So you have a type." He smirked.

"Doesn't everybody?" I shrugged.

I was always drawn in by his mouth and jawline. His perfectly straight teeth and that top lip that curls when he talks about something joyful.

"Sure, but what's yours?" He stared at me.

"I think the better question is *who* is yours?" I stood to my feet.

"What do you mean?" He smiled.

"Do you have a girlfriend?" I asked as I walked into my bathroom.

I regretted my question as soon as it passed through my lips.

"I don't do girlfriends." He chuckled.

"You're that type of guy?" I raised my eyebrow at him as I placed his like-new shirt on the bed.

Was he? Was he the type of guy to hook up with a girl and not call her back in the morning? The type my father warned me to stay away from? The type of guy to treat you like trash and throw your emotions to the side? Did I make the wrong choice befriending this guy? Was my eye candy just that?

"No." He defended himself. "Not at all. I just don't have the time. Nor have I met a girl worth calling mine."

"Yeah, I guess I get that." I nodded.

"So what about you?" He asked.

"What about me?" I leaned back on the bed.

I knew what he was hinting at but I wanted him to ask the question.

"Boyfriend?" He asked.

"The closest thing I have to a boyfriend is the human my parents are trying to marry me off to and I can't stand him." I scoffed.

"Human? Your parents are trying to set you up?" He frowned.

"Well." I caught myself. "I'm not going through with it or anything."

Although I knew I could tell him things, I needed to be careful. I had to watch what I said. I couldn't just talk loosely about my life and risk my father being reprimanded. Dimensional rules were dimensional rules and I didn't know if he was okay with someone breaking those.

"Relax." He calmed me. "I won't say anything. I get it."

"At least someone understands." I smiled.

"I completely understand." He huffed. "My father is trying to do the same."

"Why are our lives so similar Mr. Blacksfer?" I turned to face him.

As the day went on I felt more and more comfortable with him. It was like we already knew each other, we were just reconnecting. He made my freakish laugh peak and my cheeks constantly run hot. I mostly watched him. I liked watching his emotions transition. He explained his background and I took mental notes of it all. I watched as his face slowly disappeared behind my eyelids.

I woke up to hearing my door creek open and closed. Sadly, Owen was no longer by my side.

"Who's there?" I asked, looking into the darkness.

"It's me." They whispered back.

"Cat?" I flicked on the lamp beside me.

"Yes." She took off her hoodie and revealed her pretty face and long brown hair.

"How did you get in here?" I climbed out of bed and locked my door.

"Don't worry about that. I have something to tell you." She pulled me over to the bed.

"What is it?" I frowned.

"Remember when my mom died? Do you remember what your parents told you happened?" She waited for me to answer.

"Her cancer spread." I nodded.

"That was a lie." Her eyes watered.

"Why would they lie? My father loved his sister." I defended him.

"I'm not saying they are lying or that they know anything about it." She sighed. "All I'm saying is the way beings are saying she died isn't true."

"And how do you know that?" I looked at her skeptically.

"Because I was there." She admitted.

"You saw–"

"No, I came a little after." A tear fell as she stood to her feet and walked over to my window seat. "She was murdered, Xena."

"What?" I rushed over to her.

"I didn't know what to do when I saw her body there. She was face down with a blue snake branded into her wrist. I didn't know if I should call the police or just leave her there. I remember calling my father and him telling me to leave because if I was caught there I would be blamed for her death and that would destroy both her image and his." She let the tears fall.

"So you just went along with the story?" I sat next to her.

"Yes. I had to. Who would believe a middle class girl from Beauclair? They would think I was just trying to get money for her death or something." She explained. "Just keep your eyes open. Nothing is as it seems. Bad things are happening right in front of our eyes. Pay attention to the things that make you second guess yourself, it is those things that are deceiving us."

"I'm sorry. I'm just trying to grasp all of this." I shook my head in disbelief.

"Well you need to grasp it faster." She wiped her tears. "The party is over and your parents are roaming the house."

"What time is it?" I yawned.

"It's around midnight." She informed me. "Are you really listening?"

"Yes." I nodded. "Can we change the subject now? I'm scared."

"I saw you with that vamp boy today." She smirked.

"Owen?" I hid my smile.

"Yes Owen." She playfully nudged me.

"And I saw his even hotter brother Rowan." She pretended to faint.

"Everyone thinks he's cute except for me." I chuckled.

"That's because you have the hots for Owen." She nudged me again.

"He's a good friend." I corrected her.

"Sure." She drawled.

"Did you sneak back into town just to warn me?" I asked.

"Yes." She nodded. "It was something you needed to know. More blue snake deaths are happening and I had to tell you the truth. If anything ever happens to me, I did not die from some random natural cause. They killed me Xena."

"Who is doing this? Why would they want to kill you?" I frowned.

"I don't know who exactly but I'm working to find out." She sighed. "They kill those that know too much."

"Then why would you go digging around where you shouldn't be?" I asked confused.

"You still don't get it." She stood to her feet. "But you're young. I can't expect you to understand."

"I'm not that young." I pouted.

"Too young for this I'm afraid." She headed towards the door. "No one's magic is working right now. I think it's because someone is tampering with it."

She was leading me to all these doors that held information but she had no key. I couldn't do anything with the information she gave me besides worry. I needed more.

"No magic again?" I whined.

The last time our powers weren't working we had to wait six weeks before they were restored. Our entire dimension runs on magic. Without magic things start taking a turn for the worst. Besides, if I wanted my parents to go on their upcoming retreat, magic was the only way.

"So I can't practice my powers-"

"I have a source of power that I save up for times like these." She reached in her pocket and pulled out a charm anklet.

"Each charm holds a finite amount of power." She placed it on my ankle. "But no traveling through the dimensions. They can track you."

"My parents examine every accessory I wear." I watched her.

"Just say it was a gift that my mother gave you a long time ago." She stood up. "There's no way they can fact check that."

"You know I hate lying." I sighed.

"Well, which do you hate more? Lying or no magic?" She folded her arms.

"No magic." I admitted.

"Look, I'm going to be moving back here soon. I'm leaving Donny and coming back. This is where I belong. Uncle was right." She simpered.

"Are you sure that's what you want?" I placed my hand on her shoulder.

"Xena." My mother's voice echoed throughout the halls.

"Uh oh." Cat looked around the room, panicking.

"Just hide." I shooed her as I unlocked my door.

If she got caught she would be tormented and punished. I couldn't let that happen because of me. If the moment came, I would take the blame.

I heard feet shuffling towards my room.

"Hurry." I looked back to warn her but she was gone.

My window was wide open and my curtains were flowing strongly in the wind. I rushed to my window and saw her climbing into a black SUV.

"Xena." My mother knocked lightly.

I stared down at the cellphone left on my seat.

I wasn't sure if it was an accident but I didn't have time to figure that out. I shoved it into my pillowcase and climbed into bed.

"Xena, are you up?" She peeked into my room. "Xena?"

"What is it, mother?" I forced a fake yawn.

"I have to tell you something." She walked into my room leaving the door wide open.

"If you have secrets to share, you should probably pay attention to who could be listening." I mumbled.

"Our itinerary has changed." She ignored my snide.

"Meaning what exactly?" I sighed.

I didn't need any more bad news and that seemed to be all that I was getting tonight.

"The retreat got bumped up to next week and we were thinking." She walked around my room examining it.

"Thinking what?" I watched her.

"Maybe you should come with us." She hesitated.

"Mother." I groaned.

"It'll just be for a week." She sat down next to me. "There are beings sneaking into our dimension and we don't want to risk something happening to you."

"Who would want to harm the daughter of the most important being in our dimension?" I bragged. "I'll be fine."

"I – I don't think so." She shook her head.

"Besides, I meet with a recruiter that Friday." I retorted.

"You do?" She hid her smile.

"I do." I nodded.

"Well then I guess you can't come." She sighed.

"Sorry." I lied happily.

"Our lives are just too hectic right now." She complained.

I sat there and let her rant because I knew she needed to. Mother and I weren't close anymore but that didn't mean I didn't still love her or want to be close. She talked about their plans for the next few months. They were completely booked every weekend, which I was happy about but of course it made her have to work overtime to convince me that she would be worried about me. I quickly explained that I knew my parents had a busy life but that's what I had Veronica for.

"Is that your fathers shirt?" She stared down at the folded shirt on my bed.

"Uh, no." I grabbed it. "It's Isis'."

"Isis wears mens dress shirts?" She raised her eyebrow at me.

"Yes." I hissed. "And I support her weird habits."

"Strange girl that Isis." She smirked before closing my door.

I released the shirt and laid down in exhaustion. I stared over at the pillow Owen was lying on and started to reminisce. Why did he leave so early? And without saying goodbye?

I grabbed the phone from underneath my pillow and climbed out of bed. I rushed over to my faulty floor board and removed my box that stayed invisible until I touched it. I moved my other belongings to the side and placed the phone inside along with my anklet.

V: ATTAINMENT

I woke up to the morning sun on my face and anxiety in my throat. Today was the day I met with the college of my dreams, or shall I say, my parents' dreams. It was the most prestigious college in the eyes of our dimension and my father's Alma Mater. For his image alone, I needed to get into Marlsgate University.

I climbed out of my bed and headed for the shower.

In my shower I thought about this meeting and how nervous I was for all of the wrong reasons. I was more nervous about messing up and disappointing my parents than I was about not getting in. I needed to ace this interview. I didn't have a choice.

I skimmed through the business attire section of my closet until I found the dry cleaners bag that was marked college interview. I peeked inside to see the most hideous outfit I owned. I quickly zipped it up and shoved it to the back of my closet. I searched for a casual, yet semi-formal outfit, tossed it on my bed, and went to seek my mother's approval.

"Mother!" I called for her as I towel dried my hair.

"Mother?" I headed down the steps.

"She's not here." An unfamiliar voice answered.

"Uh, where is she?" I asked skeptically as I reached the last step.

"She, uh, left in the middle of the night." He answered.

"Where are you?" I looked around. "Better yet, *who* are you?"

"My apologies." A white haired young man walked towards me.

"I am Devereux." He reached his hand out to greet me.

His gray eyes matched his tousled white hair perfectly and he was dressed head to toe in some type of black armor. He looked like he just stepped out of a science fiction movie. Something unreal.

"Hello." I shook his hand slowly in confusion.

"Hello Xena." He smiled.

"Where are my parents?" I asked pulling away.

"I believe they are out of town." He said following behind me.

"Out of town?" I whispered to myself. "They didn't even say bye."

"Apparently they left in the middle of the night." He informed me.

"And how do you know this?" I turned around to face him.

"Because they hired me." He shrugged.

"To do what exactly?" I folded my arms.

"I am your new mentor." He smiled wide. "Pleasure-"

"Stop." I held my hand up. "Veronica!"

"She is in the guest house moving her stuff out." He answered.

I ran through the house and out my backdoor. Veronica was placing her things in the small garage attached to the guest house.

"What are you doing?" I asked running towards her.

"Xena." She forced a smile. "I see you've met your new house guest."

"Yes." I nodded. "But what does that have to do with you?"

"He didn't tell you?" She chuckled dryly.

"Tell me what?" I grabbed her hand.

"He is taking my place in the guest house." She hissed.

"What?" I looked back at him.

"Your fathers' request. Not mine." He shrugged. "I was fine sleeping in a guest room. I tried to explain that to your *nanny* but she clearly doesn't want to hear anything I have to say."

"You're right. I don't." She continued to move her things.

"Sleeping?" I scoffed. "You live here now?"

"For the time being, yes." He nodded.

"Will someone tell me what the hell is going on?" I scowled at both of them.

"I will." They said at the same time.

"Veronica." I said, giving her the floor.

"You parents left in the middle of the night last night. They left you a magical guidance fairy to help you with your college interviews and anything else you might need in that area." She explained.

"So they kicked you out and just moved him in?" I sighed.

"Pretty much." She placed her final box in the wagon.

"Oh please, she is staying in the guest room upstairs." He chuckled.

"She was talking to me." She barked.

"And I was talking to her." He snapped back.

"Enough!" I shouted.

They both got extremely quiet and waited for me to speak.

"That's good news though V." I assured her.

"How so?" She crossed her arms.

"We always said how cool it would be for you to live in the house with me." I grinned, hoping that would ease her anger.

"Yeah, I guess you're right." She smiled. "I get to be closer to you."

"Yes and the games are in a couple of days." I reminded her.

"What games?" He stepped forward.

"Uh." I stared at Veronica hoping she would answer.

"The Onyx games." She covered for me.

"And what's-"

"It's a witch thing. You wouldn't know anything about it." She shooed him.

"Ouch." He smiled.

"So I am stuck with this guy until when exactly?" I sighed.

"You guys are *so* welcoming." He murmured.

"Your parents said that they will be returning in a few days." She ignored his comment. "That is if magic is working again by then."

"How did they get there if magic was down?" I kicked the dirt.

"They put their powers together and had enough to travel one way." She explained. "But don't worry, they left to fix it."

"Mother and I talked last night and she didn't mention anything about this." I said angrily.

"It was sudden." She shrugged. "Don't be mad at them, X."

"Too late." I turned my back against her. "So, are you supposed to be coming with me to this interview?"

"Yes." He nodded proudly. "Now, let's go through your list of-"

"So what you're not going to do is tell me what I'm going to do." I chuckled sourly.

"What do *you* want to do then?" He sighed.

"I want Veronica to go inside and unpack her things." I smiled.

She listened and wheeled her belongings towards the house.

"And you." I pointed at him. "Do your powers still work?"

"Yes." He nodded.

"Good. I want you to go inside and wait for me in the living room." I instructed him.

I watched them until they disappeared into the house.

"And I-" I glanced down at my watch. "I need to get dressed."

I rushed into the house and quickly got dressed. My parents leaving without saying a word really affected me more than it probably should've. But how could they just up and leave knowing bad things were happening in this dimension? I knew that I had this college meeting but if they cared enough for me, they would have dragged me with them despite what I said I wanted instead of leaving me defenseless with a mortal nanny and a simple guidance fairy.

As I did my hair and makeup my mind drifted to Owen.

I immediately thought of his smile. I thought of how he let me voice my opinion and supported it. He was the only being to make me feel like what I wanted mattered. I only wish that he would have given me a way to contact him. I would've insisted that he stayed here with me while my parents were gone, but I knew that if no magic was coming in, there would be no magic to let him out.

I stood there in the mirror staring at myself. Staring at the young woman that my parents created. The façade I had to live by. I was forced to be someone I didn't even know. I didn't want to have countless rules to follow while my friends were out really living their lives.

"Okay." I walked into the living room with my portfolio in hand.

"Ready to go?" He stood to his feet.

"Not exactly." I stopped him. "You cannot go anywhere with me looking like that."

"What's wrong with it?" He stared down at his armor.

"Take a look around. No one dresses like that here." I simpered.

"Well, what do you suppose I look like?" He sat back down.

I looked around my living room and grabbed a magazine from the side table. I flipped through the pages of Casual Witch Weekly. The magazine consisted of men in casual attire made formal. I flipped to the page of the guy wearing a sweater vest.

"What about him?" I showed him the picture.

"Too studious." He shook his head.

"Okay." I skimmed through the pages again.

"Him?" I stopped on a model with hair similar to his.

His eyes were light brown and his cheekbones were so defined, his lips hiding his bad boy smile. He was wearing a light gray sweater that teased his tie and white button up underneath. He had on casual blue jeans and brown boots to match.

"Fine." He snapped his fingers and transformed into an exact replica.

"How do I look?" He stared down at himself.

"Perfect." I smiled.

"Can we go now please?" He stood up. "We have about an hour to get there and it's a 45 minute drive."

"Whatever you say." I tossed him my keys.

"Wait!" Veronica stopped me.

"I'll be in the car." He looked her up and down before walking out the front door.

"Who was that?" She smiled after him.

"That was my beloved fairy." I sighed.

"Hmm." She chuckled to herself.

"Focus V." I said impatiently.

"Right." She placed her hands on my shoulders. "You can do this. This spot is yours. You've been working for this all of your life. You've already been accepted academically. Now is your time to show them that you are worthy of that decision."

"You have picked the absolute worst time for a pep talk." I sighed.

"Why? What's wrong?" She dragged me to the couch.

"I don't have time for this. I have to go." I tried to break her grip.

"He can wait." She assured me.

"My parents are supposed to be here." I admitted. "They are supposed to be the ones driving me here and telling me it is going to be okay. They are supposed to be the ones giving me that pep talk and making me feel like no matter the outcome they would be there for me but instead they left me to face this on my own. Do you know the pressure I am feeling right now? My head is about to explode."

"Okay. Breathe." She smiled. "Everything is going to be okay."

"How do you know that?" I fought my tears.

"Because your parents didn't get you here. You did. Your parents didn't take the tests for you, you did. You are the only reason why you are here right now. So the only person you need is yourself." She walked me to the door.

"Thanks V." I hugged her tight.

"Now go kill it." She held the door open for me.

Devereux was sitting in the driver's seat waiting for me.

I had almost forgotten he was in his human form now.

"I still can't get over how cute he is." She shook her head smiling.

"If you want to keep looking at him, he's sitting in there on the table. Page 22!" I walked down the front steps.

"Page 22?" She shouted after me.

"You'll understand when I'm gone." I assured her as I climbed into the car.

"So, does Veronica have a boyfriend?" He asked as we pulled off.

"Don't even try it." I clicked my seatbelt on.

On the drive I thought about tanking this meeting intentionally just to upset my parents the way that they've upset me. I wanted to hurt them back, tarnish their image. I wanted to make them pay. Make them return home and show me the attention that I deserved and if that meant negatively then I would take that. Whatever it took to make me important again, I would do it.

"Are you ready for this?" He looked over at me as we parked.

"Yes." I nodded. "No."

"So you aren't." He turned the car off.

"I mean, we are meeting at a Café. That's pretty casual right?" I bit my lip.

"Well, it's more of an intimate yet public setting. If he took you to a conference room, it would be different but because he took you to a Café he wants to see how you react under pressure. He knows that beings will be listening and that you are a valuable asset to this dimension. Beings love you and reporters will be listening. He is testing you." He explained with a smile.

"Great." I groaned as I climbed out of the car.

"But it will be fine." He joined my side as I stared up at the building.

The sign read Impresso Espresso. By the looks of it, it was definitely high class.

"I'll be with you every step of the way." He smiled.

"Thank you." I sighed.

"Don't get distracted by my suddenly good looks though." He rubbed his face playfully.

"I won't." I rolled my eyes playfully.

"Deep breath." He pulled the door open for me.

As soon as we stepped in, the smell of cinnamon rolls and fresh coffee beans filled my senses.

"Good morning, welcome to ImpEs." A ditzy blonde girl greeted us.

"I swear that's not what I read on the sign." Devereux looked around jokingly.

"Oh, yeah I know." She laughed as she grabbed our menus. "It's just my way of pulling my laziness into my job without getting fired and besides it's much easier to say." She smirked at him. "What's your name?"

"Dev-"

"We don't have time for this." I pulled him away.

"Xena!" Four young girls rushed up to us.

"Hi." I smiled down at them.

"Can we have your autograph?" The littlest one held up a receipt and a pen.

"Sure." I smiled as I glanced at the clock.

I quickly scribbled my signature and passed it back. I rushed past the busy tables and towards the empty booths in the back.

"Excuse me young lady." A man stepped in front of me.

"Yes?" I asked looking over his shoulder for my interviewer.

"You in a rush?" He chuckled.

"Just a little." I said impatiently.

"Well, I just wanted to ask what you think about the cinnamon rolls here?" He stared at me.

"Oh, mhm. They are great. I gotta go." I rushed past him rudely.

"Is that him?" Devereux asked beside me.

There was a man sitting at a booth all alone. He was looking down at the menu confused.

"I – I think so." I fixed my hair.

"Okay, kill it." He smiled.

"Sir." I approached him.

"Oh, hello." He smiled up at me.

"Marlsgate University?" I smiled.

"Yes?" He answered.

"Hello, I'm Xena Briarwood. Pleased to meet you." I reached my hand out to shake his.

"The pleasure is mine." He shook my hand. "So what can I help you with?"

"What do you mean? Aren't you the recruiter for MU?" I blushed.

"Uh, I'm afraid not. That would be that man over there." He pointed.

He was pointing to the man who I just rudely dismissed. His hair was dark brown and slicked back perfectly. Not one hair out of place. He sat with so much poise, so much confidence. Anyone could tell he was a man of business. He was rifling through papers and typing on his phone. I looked back at Devereux awkwardly.

"Honest mistake." Devereux smiled at me. "Go."

I nervously walked over to him trying to hide the true embarrassment I felt.

"Hello, I'm Xena Briarwood. Pleased to meet you." I said shyly.

"Hello Xena. I'm Zoru." He shook my hand. "Please, sit down."

"Okay." I slid into the booth swiftly.

"Are you okay?" He smiled at me.

"Yes, I'm fine." I nodded once. "Just a little embarrassed."

"Why?" He stared down at my shaking hands.

"I mistook someone else for you." I sighed.

"In all fairness, you didn't know what I looked like and the way I approached you it was easy to assume I was just a mere customer in your way." He assured me.

"Thank you for understanding." I blushed.

"Thank you for passing the test." He smiled.

"Hello, I'm Margaret, your server." A red haired woman approached us with her notepad and pen floating behind her. "What can I get for you two today?"

"Where's my notepad?" She said feeling her apron pockets.

"Uh." I pointed to her objects floating behind her.

"Behind you." Zoru smiled.

"Oh." She turned around and grabbed her supplies.

"I guess I'm kinda lucky that they do that or else I would be buying new pens and notepads every day." She joked. "So what would you like?"

"I will have the breakfast plate with black coffee and wheat toast." He handed her back her menu.

"And for you dear?" She looked at me.

"I will just take an espresso de wander?" I chose the first thing I saw.

"Good choice. Would you be operating any machinery in the next couple of hours, Sugar?" She scribbled in her notepad.

"Uh, no." I shook my head.

"Perfect. So one espresso de wander and a breakfast plate with black coffee and wheat toast." She repeated the order.

"Yes." We said in sync.

"Okay." She giggled. "And are you ready to eat now?"

"Is it ready now?" He asked skeptically.

"Actually yes." She snapped her fingers twice and his meal appeared in front of him.

"Now that's what I call fast food." He chuckled. "This looks fantastic."

"Your espresso will be here shortly." She smiled. "They take a little longer than everything else."

"Can I ask you where you're from? Your accent is so deep." I stopped her from leaving.

"5th dimension. Everyone talks differently there." She whispered.

"That really exists?" I whispered back.

"Yes. I spent my whole life there, I moved here about a year ago." She nodded.

"That's amazing." I smiled at her.

"I think I see your espresso coming." Zoru chuckled.

I peeked down the aisle to see my drink floating towards us.

"This entire place is ran off of magic isn't it?" I smirked. "But how? Our magic isn't working."

"All major places have a generator." She shrugged.

"Thank you." I dismissed her.

"You are passing all my tests I see." He smiled as my cup placed itself on the table in front of me.

"You're testing me already?" I said nervously.

"I've been testing you since you walked through the door." He smiled.

"Great." I forced a smile back.

"So are you ready to be interrogated?" He smirked down at his paperwork.

"Is that a trick question?" I sipped my drink.

"Yes. Yes it is." He smiled up at me.

Zoru was oddly handsome, like a Barbie doll or a model. You wouldn't have ever guessed that he was a recruiter for a university this large. Maybe he was forced to work for the school, like his father owned it and gave him no other choice. As if he spent his whole life working for something he didn't even want. Or was that just me? Was he actually happy with his career? Was I the only miserable one?

"Alright." He cleared his throat, distracting me from my thoughts. "Ready for the first question?"

"Yes." I nodded confidently.

"Just remember. You should feel comfortable with me. I am just a recruiter, not your boss. I'm just here to see if your answers meet our requirements and pass that information along to Mr. Alvarez. He is the one to fear, not me." He sipped his coffee. "Understand?"

"Understood." I nodded.

"Question number one." He sighed. "How do you define success?"

"For our dimension or myself?" I answered.

"I want to hear both." He picked up his pen.

Speaking for the entire 4th dimension was a no brainer, I could do that in front of a million recruiters and reporters with no problem. It was talking about myself, the real me, that was a challenge.

"To our dimension, success means having money. If you have money you are automatically deemed successful. You could be an undercover killer, con-artist, or arsonist. Anything. Seems like as long as you have money and keep your image intact you are accepted."

"And for you?" He looked up at me.

"Success has more to do with how *you* feel about your accomplishments, not how others see you; setting goals for yourself and doing your best to meet those goals." I paused before I lied. "I was taught growing up that-"

"I don't want to hear about that. I want to hear what you feel." He stopped me.

"Honestly?" I took a deep breath and felt my feelings taking over for a second. "I feel like no matter your profession or situation in life, whether you are a toilet cleaner, car washer, even a dishwasher, life is about making the best of what you have and always moving forward with a goal in mind. Following through with your aspirations and dreams, even if you don't get to the top. You've worked hard to succeed and that's what really matters."

"You are not very fond of our dimension are you?" He chuckled.

"Off the record, no. Not at all." I answered honestly.

"Question number two. How would you describe yourself to someone who did not know you?" He hid his smile.

How can someone possibly describe who they are to someone else when they don't even know who they are themselves? I don't know who I am. All I know is what my parents have instilled in me. I had all the right answers to all of his questions but were they answers that I believed in?

"I would describe myself as a quiet, intelligent, deep thinker who is full of untapped potential and may be purposely hampered by those around her out of fear." I spoke with confidence.

"Fear of what?" He looked up at me.

"Annihilation." I smirked.

"I agree. I see a fire in you that reminds me of myself. I can see it in your eyes. You want freedom, you long for freedom." He spoke passionately.

"Yes I do." I admitted.

"Then why is it that are you still trapped? Maybe it is *you* that is afraid." He challenged me with a smirk.

"Next question." I cleared my throat.

"Why are you interested in us?" He flipped through some pages.

"I am interested in your college because it's all I've ever dreamed of. I've been collecting brochures from your campus since I was 6 years old and my father used to teach there after he graduated-"

"Brice Briarwood." He grinned.

"What? You know him?" I asked confused. "Personally, I mean?"

"Very well actually." He chuckled as he scribbled something illegible on paper.

"How?" I tried to subtly read his notes.

"He was my teacher." He chuckled. "I used to give him such a hard time my freshman year."

"Wait. How old are you?" I questioned him.

"You do the math." He sipped his drink.

"Well my father started to teach when I was eight. I'm seventeen now. You said freshman year. So that would make you twenty-six?" I smiled.

"Guilty." He smiled back.

"Wow. I thought you were so much older." I stared at him.

"Yeah, stress has a great way of making you regret things." He admitted.

"I didn't mean it like that. I meant with your profession." I corrected myself.

"Just taking over for my father." He nodded.

"I know what that feels like." I mumbled.

"Proudest achievement so far?" He ignored my comment.

"It would have to be my stellar grades and outstanding attendance. I wasn't really allowed to do sports or extra-curriculars. My grades are all I really had. Which I don't regret because it got me where I am. I love to read. I've been reading above college level since I was ten years old. I've always stood out in my group of my friends. I am the one everyone comes to for advice. I've also learned how to read beings very well." I spoke confidently.

"Read me." He said with a hint of flirtation in his voice.

"Well." I cleared my throat and began examining him.

"Well?" He said impatiently.

"Your parents are beyond wealthy. You are most likely the baby of the family. The last one to polish your dad's name to perfection before it reaches the wall of fame. No pressure." I smirked. "You have a kid. Maybe two. Everyone always looks at you as the irresponsible one. That new Porsche in the first parking spot is yours and by the looks of what you ordered, you are a newly divorced man."

"Wow." He blinked slowly. "Wow."

"Am I right?" I smiled.

"Spot on." He laughed. "I've got to give it to you Xena, you will definitely be a valuable asset to MU."

"Thank you." I nodded.

"Honestly, I know you will answer the rest of my questions perfectly so I'm going to skip through and ask you one last question." He put down his pen.

"Okay." I smiled excitedly.

"What do you think of the cinnamon buns here? Are they any good?" He winked playfully.

"I think they are great." I played along.

"And that concludes our meeting for today." He packed his papers in his suitcase and pulled out a rosemary colored envelope. "You know what these are right?"

"Acceptance or denial letters." I answered.

"Yes." He nodded. "Open it at exactly midnight and your answer will appear. If you don't, your letter will self-destruct into ashes."

"No pressure." I said sarcastically.

"None at all." He joked as he flagged down our waiter.

"Yes?" She smiled.

"Cinnabun to go?" He tossed his halo-card on the table.

Halo-cards were holographic credit cards that were linked to your bank account. They were translucent with your signature across them and golden stars to show off your wealth. It was just another way for beings to know your social status without asking.

"It's already in your car and ready to go." She smiled.

She ran his card under the scanner in her hand and returned it.

"Thank you." He stood to his feet and collected his things.

"Xena." He reached his hand out to shake mine. "It was nice to meet you."

"Likewise." I nodded.

"Keep in touch." He placed his business card on the table.

"I will." I slid it in my pocket.

"Stay beautiful." He walked away.

I sat there for a few seconds, staring down at the envelope.

"Tell me everything." Devereux slid into the empty seat.

"Everything went great." I smiled.

"Really?" He grinned.

"Yeah. I even think he was flirting with me a little bit." I bit my lip.

"That's a good sign." He laughed.

"I know." I shrieked.

"I mean, I know." I said again calmly.

"I gotta get home and tell V." I pulled him from his seat.

"Wait." He stopped me.

"What?" I asked confused.

"Let's sit and talk for a while." He smiled.

"About what?" I folded my arms.

VI: AMOUR PROPRE

We talked for hours, just getting to know each other. He wasn't the prude I thought he was, although I was still unsure of which dimension he came from. Was it possible he was from the 5th dimension? After we stuffed ourselves full of cinnamon rolls, we headed home.

"V!" I ran into my dark house.

Everything was still as if no one had been there for years. My house was never pitch black. There were always lights, a record playing, or servants around. Something wasn't right.

"Whoa." Devereux walked in. "Where is everybeing?"

"I – I don't know." I felt around for a light switch.

"Times like these don't you wish you had your mag-"

"Surprise!" Beings shouted as the lights came on.

All of my friends were here and many familiar faces from school. As much as I appreciated Isis, this was completely inappropriate.

"Congratulations!" She hugged me.

"This is so nice of you but V is going to kill me." I whispered.

"I doubt that." She giggled.

Veronica stepped out of the crowd and walked over to us.

"You like?" She looked around.

"V." I smirked. "You knew?"

"Of course I knew." She chuckled.

"She planned, we showed." Zoe and Sarai joined our mini circle.

"Z, S." I smiled.

"Congratulations." They both kissed my cheek.

"Thank you!" I shrieked.

"Where's L?" I looked around.

"She and Lisa were supposed to be here but you know how Lisa is." Sarai rolled her eyes.

"Oh, how rude are we?" Sarai smiled over at Devereux. "I'm sorry we just left you on the porch like that. I didn't even know you were standing there."

"Hey." He waved at her.

"Come in." She pulled him gently by his arm. "Want a drink?"

"Uh, sure." He shrugged as she pulled him into the kitchen.

"Drinks?" I looked at V. "I had no idea they would be bringing drinks. I can go handle that right now. I-"

"Xena." She sighed. "It's okay. I haven't seen anything."

"But-"

"In fact, I think this cup of punch is yours." She placed the full cup in my hand.

"Oh, no thank you. I don't drink." I smiled.

"Of course you don't." She smirked. "Drink up."

"No seriously-"

"No seriously, drink up." She replied.

"Come on Xena. To senior year!" Isis raised her cup.

"Yes, to senior year!" V placed her cup in the air. "Well, your senior year."

I looked around at all the supportive faces in front of me. The beings that really loved me back. The beings that would do anything and everything for me. The ones I wouldn't be with anymore next year. It was the end of our chapter. It had to be memorable, it had to be perfect.

"To senior year!" I shouted as we clunked our plastic cups together.

The pink alcohol slid down my throat like a slushy on a hot summer day. It tasted so sweet yet so vile. It sent a cold chill down my spine that instantly made my knees weak. I pulled the cup from my lips to see everyone still drinking. I waited for them to be done.

"Brain freeze." Isis smiled as she rubbed her temples.

"Aw. Me too." Zoe groaned.

"Not me." V smiled proudly.

"Your Nanny is so cool." Zoe shrieked. "Can you be my nanny?"

"Sorry Zoe. I only serve one kid." Veronica pulled me away.

"Where are we going?" I asked, laughing.

"You are going to go get changed. It's your celebration party!" She pulled me up the stairs and into her guest room.

"So I was thinking this red dress with these black heels." She laid the red satin dress on her bed and placed tall black heels beside it.

"This? For me?" I hesitated.

"Yes Xena." She sighed. "Why not? Because Mommy and Daddy say you can't wear anything above your knees? Because you can't show anything appealing right?"

"Right." I nodded.

"Take a look around. Mommy and Daddy aren't here and I am in charge of you. I say what goes. So if I have to force you to have fun I will. Now put the dress on." She ordered.

"Fine." I smiled as I stripped out of my clothing.

A part of me knew what V was doing was wrong but the other part of me didn't care. She was right. I deserved this.

I slipped into the tight dress that fit me like a hug. Just by the smell of the dress I could tell it was expensive and definitely this seasons. The sleeves stopped half way down my arm and the dress stopped in a flow, mid-thigh. The back of the dress was an inch or two longer than the front and the black heels made me go from 5'2 to 5'5 instantly. Their red bottoms complimented my dress while the top of the shoe matched my purse down to the white stitching in the buckle.

"This dress was made for you." She smiled.

"Can I see?" I walked towards the mirror.

"Not yet." She pulled me back. "My masterpiece isn't done yet."

"So, how was Devereux?" She asked as she painted my face.

"What do you mean?" I tried to hide my discomfort.

"How was his company on your interview?" She rephrased.

"Oh, he is a good supporter." I nodded.

"That's good." She hissed.

"Why?" I opened one eye to look at her.

"Why what?" She pretended not to know what I was talking about.

"V." I drawled.

"What?" She huffed.

"Stop stalling." I opened one eye. "Do you think he's cute or something?"

"I think he's okay." She nodded.

"Just okay?" I smirked.

"Yes. Just okay." She pulled away. "What is this? 21 questions?"

"Kinda." I chuckled.

"All done." She stood back to look at me.

"So, can I see now?" I smiled.

"Sure." She put her makeup away.

I stepped into the light above the mirror and examined myself. My cleavage was showing, my legs were fully exposed, and my shoes alone were violating dress code. I began to doubt myself as my smile faded into a worried look.

"What's wrong? You look beautiful." She rubbed my shoulders.

"They will never find out right?" I bit my lip.

"Never." She whispered.

I stared down at my full cup and placed it to my lips. I chugged it until I felt my throat rejecting the taste.

"Xena." V grabbed my arm concerned.

"Don't call me that, not tonight." I swallowed.

"Okay then." She chuckled. "What should I call you?"

"Nyomi." I walked out.

I looked over the staircase at all of my guests.

They all looked happy, so relaxed. Having fun like normal teenagers. I needed to learn to be like them. I needed to learn to be free.

"Xena." Isis spotted me.

She waved her hands in the air so I could find her but my eyes were already locked in her area.

"Come here." She mouthed to me as she danced with Niko.

Niko and Isis dated back when we were freshman. I knew for a fact she wasn't dating him again, Isis wasn't the type to double dip. So if she was entertaining him it was probably because she wanted something. Isis always had a way of getting what she wanted.

I skipped down the stairs and through the crowds of beings trying to talk to me. I heard whispers about my appearance that boosted my blossoming ego. I squeezed through the crowd until I was standing right in front of Isis and Niko who were dancing all over each other.

"You look great." She examined me.

"Thank you." I smiled back.

"Really great." Niko added.

"She gets it." Isis rolled her eyes playfully as she sipped her drink.

"So." Isis smiled. "Like the party?"

"Love the party." I pulled her cup away from her.

She was visibly drunk and I didn't want her to get into anything.

"Hey! I wasn't done with that." She whined.

"You are now." I finished the cup.

"I heard Lisa invited beings from other dimensions." She informed me.

"She what?" I asked furiously.

"Yeah. She said something about spicing it up." She shrugged, still dancing.

"Actually, here they come now." She pointed to the opening door.

My heart skipped a beat as I saw a familiar face walking towards me. I wasn't sure if he was looking at me or looking past me. As the butterflies filled my stomach, my anxiety started to kick in. I quickly chugged the cups from the trusted beings around me as he made his way through the crowd.

"Xena, what is it?" Zoe tried to read my expression.

"Huh?" I asked pretending not to hear her.

"He's here." I shrieked.

"Owen?" Isis smiled. "Did he bring his hot brother?"

"Hey." Niko complained as she pushed him away.

"I don't know. I'm not looking." I nervously turned my back to him.

"X, relax." Zoe smiled. "Here. Take my cup."

"Thank you." I smiled before drinking it empty.

"Whoa, slow down." Isis pulled the cup from my mouth.

"I don't feel anything yet." I groaned.

"It's all going to hit you at once." She warned. "There's a little something else in there too."

I searched for familiar faces that I could steal from. I would do anything to shake my nerves at this point. Owen was here and I couldn't let him see me this apprehensive.

"I don't care." I stole Devyn's cup.

"Hey Xena, looking good tonight." He flirted.

"Not now Devyn." I sighed.

"Come find me by the end of the night, yeah?" He winked before being pulled into a dance.

"Uh, I think he's coming over here." Zoe nudged me.

"Really?" I glanced over at her.

"Really." She smiled as she watched him.

I took a deep breath in and when I turned around, Owen was standing a few feet away from me making unbreakable eye contact.

"Xena." Veronica stepped in front of me, forcing me to break our stare to meet hers.

"Yes?" I said, trying to hide my smile.

I tuned Veronica's voice out as the room started to spin slowly and the familiar faces started to blur together. I could still feel Owen's eyes on me as I tried to stay focused.

"Are you listening to me?" She asked impatiently.

"What? Yeah." I lied.

"Are you drunk?" She questioned me. "I gave you one cup."

"No, I'm not drunk." I giggled. "You were saying?"

"I was saying that I'm going to turn in for the night." She smiled. "If you need me I'll be in the guest house."

"The guest house?" I questioned her.

"Ready?" Devereux walked up and put his arm around her shoulder.

"Uh, yeah." She blushed.

"Oh, hey Xena." He smiled at me.

"Hi." I stared at V.

"We will discuss your next college meeting in the morning." He said before they turned and walked away.

"Hey, he was mine!" Sarai whined as she walked up. "Whatever. He seemed a little gay anyway."

"Sarai." I scolded her.

"What? I'm drunk." She shrugged. "Can we go get more drinks?"

"Let's go." Zoe pulled Sarai through the crowd.

"Hey Owen." Isis smiled at him. "Where's Rowan?"

I swallowed hard and waited for his response.

"He's at home. This isn't his scene." He laughed.

"That's too bad." She frowned.

"Not really." A white haired boy chimed in. "I'm way more fun."

"I like the sound of that." Isis smirked.

"Can I escort you to get a drink?" He asked, holding out his arm.

"Definitely." Isis pulled away from Niko and walked away with her new date.

"Xena." Owen smiled warmly.

Just the sound of his voice made me sober up. I couldn't believe he was standing right in front of me. He was here to celebrate my day with me and I couldn't let him down. My anger towards Lisa quickly shifted to a grateful feeling.

"Owen." I smiled back.

"We gotta stop meeting like this." He chortled.

"If I didn't know any better I'd say you were stalking me, Mr. Blacksfer." I said with a hint of flirtation in my voice.

"Stalking, no. But I am *very* happy to be here." He flirted back.

The room began to spin as I searched for the real version of Owen instead of the many versions that surrounded him. Isis was right. Whatever this was, hit me all at once. I stared down at my feet trying to focus my eyes.

"I- I don't feel so good." I said trying to keep balance.

Before I knew it, Owens' arm was around my waist keeping me balanced.

"Can I take you somewhere to sit?" He spoke softly.

I held my breath as his face was now a few inches from mine.

"Hey Xena, you okay?" Dax approached us.

"Yeah she's okay." Owen said with his arm still around me. "Right Xena?"

"Yeah, I'm fine." I smiled up at him.

"Who is this guy? Is he your date?" Dax asked jealously.

"Who's asking?" Owen said seriously.

"You haven't heard? We're getting married." He smiled.

"What? No we are not." I slurred.

"She's just drunk right now. She knows we are." He smiled.

"If she's your future wife then why is she still in my arms?" Owen challenged him.

"Enough!" I drunkenly broke free from Owens' grip and stumbled between them. "No fighting."

"Can you please take me to sit down?" I sighed.

"Sure." Dax stepped up to me.

"Not you." I stumbled over to Owen.

"Of course I will." He grabbed my hand and led me out of the crowd.

"What?" Dax threw his hands in the air.

"See ya." Owen smirked back at him.

I directed Owen to my father's study. If this was what being drunk felt like, it was going to be a while before I drank again. I didn't want Owen to think I was just some party girl that gets ridiculously drunk and gets hit on by guys all night. That was exactly what it looked like. I needed to prove to him that's not what it was. I just did this to shake the nerves of being around *him*.

We walked into the dark study. Owen closed the door behind us and turned on the desk lamp. I grabbed the mahogany colored blanket that draped over the couch and sat down with it in my lap. He leaned back against the wooden desk staring at me. I didn't mind his stare. I didn't feel insecure or awkward. He brought out a sense of confidence in me. Something that was very much needed.

"So, on a scale of 1-10 how drunk are you right now?" He grinned.

"Right now?" I pretended to contemplate it. "I'd say about 11."

"Can I ask why you drank so much? Have you ever been drunk before?" He folded his arms.

"Honestly, no." I sighed. "I hope I haven't given you that impression."

"No, not all. I'm just glad I got to you before your future husband did." He smirked.

"Thank you for that." I smiled. "You can go back to the party if you want. I'll be fine here."

"Now why would I do that?" He frowned.

"You came all this way. I'm sure you don't want to be stuck in this stuffy room with a drunk girl." I smiled wryly.

"Trust me I prefer it." He admitted flirtatiously.

My heart dropped as he matched the response I wanted perfectly. It was like he had all the right answers. I knew it wasn't right for me to look at him the way I did but I could shake the feeling he gave me.

"In that case." I walked over to the fireplace and ignited the fire.

The sweet smell of the sage scented wood filled the room in seconds. I slid my heels off and sat down on the couch again.

"Sit with me?" I smiled up at him.

"How are you feeling?" He asked as he sat down next to me.

"Better now." I blushed.

"So what is this party for?" He asked curiously.

"I pretty much got accepted to the college of my dreams. So Veronica decided to throw a surprise party for me." I explained.

I watched as he made himself comfortable on the couch. I loved how he always made himself comfortable.

"Tell me all about it." He smiled at me.

"Well, getting into MU is a generational accomplishment. My father went there, his father, and even his father. Being the only child, I am next in line to follow through. MU focuses mostly on magic. You don't really have to learn much as far as studies go. MU prepares you for the trials you may face as being a young witch or wizard. It's the highest ranked school in my dimension. If you get in, you are destined for greatness and well, I got in." I smiled back.

"Sounds like more of your fathers' dream than yours." He pointed out.

"Well, according to my parents there's not much of a difference." I sighed.

"Why do you always refer back to them like that?" He grabbed my chin. "What kind of hold do they have on you?"

"A strong one." I admitted.

"Can I help you?" He said with his face just inches from mine.

"How?" I struggled to answer.

"You'll see." He stood to his feet. "You just have to say that you trust me."

"Why?" I stood firmly to mine. "Why should I trust you?"

"Why so many questions?" He brushed my cheek lightly.

"Why such unreadable answers?" I embraced his touch.

Unlike the stories I've heard about vampires being ice cold and rock hard, he had more of a warm feeling with a cool touch. Warm enough to soothe me but cool enough to send chills throughout my body. I didn't know if it was the alcohol but I was definitely enjoying the vibe coming from Owen.

"Are you the type to read into everything I say?" He chuckled.

"No, I'm just the type to want direct answers." I corrected him.

"I like that." He flirted.

"I bet." I pulled away.

"You know those heels really add to your height." He looked down at them. "Kind of deceiving really."

"What? You don't like short girls?" I raised my eyebrow at him.

"I don't really have a type, if I like you I like you." He shrugged.

"So are you saying you like me?" I smirked.

"Tell me more about MU." He tried to change the subject.

As much as I wanted that question answered, I didn't pry. I wanted to know if the feelings were mutual but now wasn't the time. As the night went on it would be obvious what page he was on.

"No, let's talk about you." I smiled.

"Anything." He nodded.

"How can I get information out of you?" I asked as I walked around the room.

"Lets play 21 questions." I suggested.

"Okay." He smirked.

"What's your biggest fear?" I challenged him.

"My biggest fear would have to be." He paused. "Losing another member of my family."

"Who did you lose, if you don't mind me asking?" I said sympathetically.

"My mother." He admitted. "Few years back."

"I'm so sorry Owen." I rubbed his hand.

"It's fine." He shook the sadness from his expression. "Next question?"

"What do you aspire to be?" I smiled at him.

"I plan to take over my father's company and open new branches." He sighed.

"Sounds more like your fathers' dream than yours." I mocked him.

"Touché." He chuckled.

The next few hours passed by so fast they felt like seconds. With Owens' laugh and compliments ringing in my ear it was hard for me to watch the time. The butterflies did not leave my stomach not even once. He asked questions about me no one else seemed to care about. He asked about my likes, my dislikes, my allergies, even my pet peeves. It was clear that Owen Blacksfer was definitely into Xena Briarwood.

I looked out at the dark sky lit up by the fireflies and resting stars.

"The sky is so beautiful tonight." I smirked.

"Do you want to get a closer look?" He reached for my hand.

"Sure." I met his reach.

We walked out of the study and through the house. Majority of the beings were gone besides my friends and a few others that were passed out drunk. Isis was laying on the couch making out with Owen's friend from earlier. I smiled as I passed them knowing Isis would have a story to tell me in the morning. We walked out onto my porch where we were greeted by the midnight moon and friendly fireflies. We walked down my steps as my porch swing swayed gently in the wind. I giggled as the damp grass tickled my feet.

"Want to look at the stars?" I plopped down in the grass.

"Yes. Do you do this often?" He sat next to me.

"Yes." I laid back and stared up at the stars.

The smell of grass made my nose tickle. It reminded me of the days when I used to play in the back yard with Aunt Cyn. We used to laugh and chase fireflies until the sun peeked over the cliffs and the fireflies faded away. Those were the best times I could remember.

"What about you?" I smiled.

"I used to do it with my mother. I haven't lately." I could hear the sadness in his voice.

I grabbed his hand, letting him know I was there.

"We can do it together now if you want." I sat up.

"I'd like that." He chuckled. "You know what else I like?"

"What?" I stared over at him.

"You." He leaned in.

I met his reach as if a magnet was pulling me. The yellow bugs danced around us lightly as our lips met. And just like that, I was happy. I didn't have one negative emotion in my body.

VII: ONEIRISM

My footprints followed me steadily across the sand as I made my way down to the shore. The smell of the sea tickled my nose and I could almost taste the salt on my tongue. I'd never seen something more gorgeous than that mass of sapphire blue stretching to the farthest ends of what my eyes could see, almost as if it were trying to kiss the orange sun. I smiled as my eyes locked on something washing up with the waves. I reached for the glossy pink shell and ran my fingers over its smooth surface.

"Xena!" Owen shouted from the terrace of our beachfront home.

"Coming!" I shouted back.

With one last glance at the sinking sun, I tucked the shell into my pocket and made my way back up the beach.

"Did you find anything?" He lifted me onto the terrace and greeted me with a kiss.

"Just this." I showed him the prize from my pocket.

"She'll love it." He assured me.

"Where is she?" I asked as he wrapped his arms around mine.

"She's down for a nap." He nibbled on my ear.

"Perfect." I pulled him into the house by his hand.

"How was your night?" Veronica said waking me up from my dream.

"Well, good morning to you too." I yawned.

"No, seriously how was your night?" She asked eagerly. "Actually, no. You can tell me everything over breakfast."

"What time is it?" I groaned as my ears began to ring.

"7:30." She answered before walking out.

"It is spring break you know!" I shouted after her.

"Don't care. Shower. Now." She ordered.

This was my second week out of school and so far I've only met with one recruiter and my set goal was five. If I wanted to be the best I had to strive for it. I just wish that Owen wasn't my every other thought so maybe I could focus.

"Xena." Dev's voice echoed over my intercom as I got dressed.

"Yes?" I turned the volume down.

"You have a meeting at 12." He chewed.

"Fantastic. Where is it?" I smirked.

"Here." He replied.

"You didn't think to tell me that?" I groaned.

"I just did." He scoffed. "V wants you downstairs for breakfast."

"Coming." I sighed.

Good thing I picked out the perfect outfit for an interview. Mother and Father would be proud of my attire. I just wish they were here to be proud of me. I stood at the top of my stairs looking down at what used to be trashed but was now a perfectly spotless foyer. I quickly rushed down the stairs with my portfolio in hand.

"V!" I called out.

"Kitchen!" She answered back.

As soon as I reached the last step I could smell pancakes and some sort of meat being fried. Food that Mother and Father would never allow.

"Good morning." I walked into the kitchen. "Well, officially."

"Good morning." They moved around each other awkwardly.

"Who cleaned up for me?" I ignored their body language.

"Me." Dev answered.

"Him." Veronica nodded.

"What's going on?" I sat down at the bar.

"What do you mean?" Veronica plated my food.

"Yeah, what do you mean?" Dev flashed a fake smile.

"Nothing I guess." I shrugged.

The vibe between them was weird. It was like they were avoiding contact with another. I watched in silence until I couldn't take it anymore.

"Okay seriously." I growled. "Someone tell me what's going on."

"Breakfast." Veronica pushed my plate in front of me. "Eat up."

"Breakfast is the most important meal of the day." Dev added.

"He's right." She nodded as she nervously washed the dishes.

"What do you mean he's right? V, you don't even eat breakfast." I chewed.

"Doesn't mean it's not important." She corrected me.

"It isn't to you because if it was, you'd be eating it." I argued.

"Okay Xena, We get it. I don't eat breakfast." She sighed.

"I mean it's okay to skip sometimes." Dev defended her.

"Okay, what the hell?" I pushed my plate away.

"Xena!" Veronica scolded me.

"Did you two hook up last night or something?" I asked jokingly.

"What? No. That's absurd. Why would you ask such a thing?" She answered defensively.

"Because that's how you both are acting." I chuckled dryly.

They glanced at each other and then back at me.

"You did, didn't you?" I smiled. "Did I just walk into the morning after?"

"Xena, I-"

"It's okay. Me and my breakfast can go upstairs." I hopped off the barstool with my food in hand.

"Xena, wait!" Veronica called after me.

"No thank you!" I walked out of the kitchen.

The portal door opened and my parents stepped out.

"Xena." My mother rushed towards me.

"Hello mother." I smiled at her.

"You do not need to be eating that." She stole the plate from me and passed it back to my father. "Here take this energy bar I got from the 1st dimension."

She handed me a small bar in a green wrapper.

"Thanks." I stared down at my new breakfast.

"How was the meeting with MU?" My father asked as he ate my plate.

Now you care?

"It was great." I smiled.

"That's excellent." He smiled back. "Where's your letter? I want to read it."

"It's upstairs. I'll go get it." I rushed up the stairs.

I stopped at the top of the stairs so I could hear what they were going to say about me. Good or bad I needed to hear it.

"I'm so proud of her." Mother started.

"This will look great on paper. We have to call Witch Weekly and tell them that our daughter got into MU." His voice echoed up the stairs. "Dimensional leader Brice Briarwoods' daughter makes good. I can see the papers now!" He exclaimed.

"I'll have Veronica get on that now." She agreed.

"Xena, where's that letter?" He said impatiently.

"It's coming!" I shouted back.

I ran in my room and quickly picked up my purse from my vanity chair. I searched for my rosemary letter but it was nowhere in sight. All that was left was ash all over my belongings.

"At midnight it will self-destruct." I heard Zoru's voice in my head.

I knew Mother and Father would be disappointed in the physical proof but once I told them about how great the interview went I'm sure they would understand.

"Okay so, we might have a small problem." I sighed.

"What? Where's the letter?" My father asked frantically.

"It self-destructed." I admitted.

"Oh, Xena." My mother shook her head.

"But, I'm 99.9% positive I got in. The recruiter even said so himself." I assured them.

"It's true. I was there." Devereux backed me up.

A swift knock at the door cut off my father's response.

"Who is that?" He asked as he stormed towards the door.

"That would be OC's recruiter." Devereux answered.

"OC?" I asked excitedly.

Overton College was the college that I personally wanted to get into. It was all paid, dorm living, magic-free learning. That's what I needed. I didn't want to focus on magic all the time and it wasn't like I was practicing it at MU, I was just studying it.

"Great." My father ditched his plate into the planter.

"Brice." My mother frowned.

"Veronica will get it." He fanned her complaint before opening the door.

"Hello Sir." A tall man stood in my opened doorway.

"Hello." My father shook his hand firmly. "Vincent, is it?"

"Well, yes it is." He nodded. "And you must be Xena?"

"Yes, Hello." I shook his hand.

"Shall we begin?" He smiled at me.

"Father. Where should we sit?" I looked around.

"My study is fine." He answered. "Follow me."

As my father led us into his study, I remembered flashbacks of that night with Owen. His hand against my cheek, his lips against mine. I couldn't help but miss him. I wanted him.

"Do you mind if I stay?" My father asked us as we sat down.

"Well uh, Xena, do you?" The recruiter looked for my answer.

I shrugged hoping he would just deny his request and kick him out but that was the opposite of what happened.

"Sure." He smiled.

"Great." My father sat next to me.

"Okay, first question." He started. "What is your set goal right now?"

"My set goal would have to be-"

"That's easy." My father cut me off. "To follow in the footsteps of the great leaders before her, right Xena?"

"No offense Mr. Briarwood, but I need Xena to answer for herself." He smiled at him, seemingly annoyed.

"Of course." My father nodded.

"Xena." Vincent started again. "What could you bring to OC that will spread positivity?"

"I-" Father tried to answer.

"I think my smarts alone bring enough to the table not to mention my outgoing personality. I love to help beings. I'm kind of a fixer. I am always willing to reach out my hand to others." I spoke over him.

I could see the annoyance building in the recruiter. I was just hoping that Father didn't ruin this for me.

"Confident. I like that." He nodded. "Now, what is your biggest fear?"

"My biggest fear would have to be losing sight of what's really important to me." I glanced over at my father.

"Such as?" He scribbled on his clipboard.

Owen.

"Such as-"

"Losing me." My father interrupted. "Xena would be devastated if she lost me. We are extremely close and that would just break her heart."

"That's it Mr. Briarwood! I cannot deal with your constant disruptions and arrogant demeanor. This is Xena's interview, not yours. Well, it was. You better start apologizing to your daughter because you just ruined her chances of getting into OC." He walked out.

I sat there for a second processing what just happened. I couldn't move, I couldn't think. I was beyond enraged.

"Xena I-"

"Don't!" I stormed out.

"Xena!" My mother called after me as I ran past her.

"What did you do, Brice?" I heard her say as I stomped up the stairs.

I closed my door and locked it behind myself. I couldn't believe he just ruined my chances of getting into the college that *I* wanted. I was starting to think that maybe that was his plan from the beginning. I was stupid to think it would've went any other way.

I climbed into my bed and cried until I couldn't anymore. I'm sure you could hear my frustrated cries echoing throughout the house. There was so much that I wanted to say but couldn't out of the respect that I still had for him. Why did I respect him so much? Was he even worthy of it? I cried until I drifted off in exhaustion.

"Hey." Isis' voice echoed throughout my room.

"X. You there? Magic is back. Hello?" She whispered again.

I climbed out of my bed, still half asleep and pulled out the trunk from under it. I unlocked it with the prick of my finger and drop of blood. I opened the trunk and pulled out two white crystals, a mixing bowl, and white rose petals.

I quickly placed my two crystals on either side of me and pulled the mixing bowl and rose pedals in front of me. As I minced the rose petals with a few drops of my blood, the crystals lit up beside me letting me know the connection was trying to be made.

"X. Can you see me?" Isis appeared across from me in holographic form.

"Yes." I nodded.

"Magic is back." She cheered.

"Clearly." I laughed. "But my parents took my board so I had to connect the old fashioned way."

"Wait. What's wrong? It looks like you've been crying." She sighed. "Who did it?"

"Your beloved Godfather." I rolled my eyes.

"Oh no, what did he do now?" She groaned.

"He sabotaged my meeting with OC." Tears filled my burning eyes.

"Intentionally-"

"I think so." I nodded.

"Okay well, I'm coming over to make you feel better." She smiled.

"It's okay, you don't have to." I smiled back.

"I'm coming." She shrugged. "I have to tell you about last night."

"Wait til you hear about mine." I bragged.

"With Owen." She teased.

"Not so loud!" I warned her.

"Sorry, sorry." She smiled. "I'll be over around 8."

"Sounds good." I nodded.

"Can Zoe and Sarai come?" She asked.

"Sure. The more the merrier, I guess." I shrugged.

"Yay! It'll be a girls night! We haven't had one in a while and I'm dying to hear one of Sarai's sex stories." She said excitedly.

"Me too." I agreed.

"Xena?" My mother called for me.

"I gotta go." I picked up one crystal breaking our visible connection.

"Okay." She sighed.

"Wait." I put the crystal back in its place. "Do you think you can get some, you know?"

"Some what?" She frowned.

"Brownies." I whispered.

"Sure. I can have my mom bake some." She smiled. "With the white chocolate chips?"

"Not that kind." I rolled my eyes.

"Oh." She nodded. "I'll see what I can do."

I shoved everything under the bed and pretended to be asleep.

"Xena." My mother walked in.

"Yes?" I pretended to stretch.

"We have a dinner to attend tonight for Gregory's birthday." She stood over me.

Gregory was Isis' father.

That's probably why she was trying to hang out tonight. Her parents wouldn't be home and neither would mine. That sneaky Isis.

"Okay." I nodded before returning to my side.

"I hope you aren't upset with your father." She sighed. "He was just trying to help."

"I don't need his help." I hissed as tears stained my pillow.

"Xena don't make me choose sides. I promise you will not like the outcome." She said before closing my door.

I spent the next few hours writing letters to Owen. Letters I would probably never give to him. Letters that explain my feelings about him, about my life currently. Things I would never have the guts to say but are so easily flowing on paper. Things I wanted to tell him about but had no way to. I placed the five letters neatly in my hidden box. I pulled out my secret cell phone and powered it on. The holographic screen appeared inches above the phone. I clicked on the contact list hoping I'd see names I recognized.

Four boxes appeared with the list of dimensions. I clicked on the 3rd.

Hundreds of names popped up and I scrolled directly to the O's. I tried to hide my smile when I saw Owen's number stored. I knew it was a risk contacting him but how would anyone find out if they didn't know of the phone's existence? I clicked his name and 'Type text here' appeared across the screen. I sat there for a moment contemplating the perfect message:

I know how risky this is but I just wanted to let you know I can't stop thinking about you. I hope we can lay under the stars together again sometime soon. My magic is finally working again. I can't wait to see you at the games as promised.

A sudden knock at my door ended my play with my new phone. I slid my box back in its hiding spot and ran downstairs to let Isis in.

"You're early." I opened the door.

"Didn't know I was invited." Dax stood drunkenly in my doorway with a bottle in his hand.

"You weren't." I crossed my arms.

"Well, can I come in?" He smiled. "Please?"

"I don't think that is such a good idea." I shook my head. "My parents aren't even home."

"They weren't home last night but that didn't stop you from dressing like a little slu-"

"Watch it." I snarled. "I don't want to hurt you Dax but I will."

"Am I supposed to be afraid of you?" He chuckled. "Now I asked if I could come in. Where are your manners?"

"Leave. Now." I ordered.

"Or what?" He stepped in.

The lights flickered off and back on. Magic was down again.

"You know what that means." He smiled back at me. "No magic. No exit for Dax."

"Why are you doing this?" I rolled my eyes.

"Who was that guy?" He questioned me.

"What guy?" I looked around.

"Don't play dumb Xena. It's very unattractive of you. That guy that had his arm around you." He stumbled towards me.

"I don't know what you're talking about." I shrugged.

"Oh you don't remember?" He placed the bottle on the ground. "Let me show you."

"Don't touch me!" I fought him.

"Like this." He forced his arm around my waist.

"Okay. You showed me. Can you please let me go now?" I begged.

"Why won't you be with me?" He tried to kiss me.

"Because. We don't belong together Dax. It isn't right. You don't want me for the right reasons." I fought him.

"Well your father seems to agree with me, and your mother agrees with anything he says. So, I win." He gloated childishly.

"It's my life, I have a say." I argued.

"Since when?" He tightened his grip.

"You're hurting me." I began to fight him again. "Let me go!"

He slammed me against the wall and pressed his body against mine.

"It's useless to fight me." He leaned in for a kiss.

I could feel the warm blood soaking my hair as my vision blurred.

"What do you want?" I turned my head away from him.

"You." He kissed my neck.

"You will never have me!" I pushed him away.

"Oh yes I will." He grabbed my face.

The lights flickered again as he forced his lips on mine. I closed my eyes and chanted the easiest spell I could think of.

"Xena!" Dax called out for me as I opened my eyes.

"Wait! I'm sorry!" He tried to fight the spell that was forcing him out.

With my head still spinning and the world still blurry, I ran frantically to the guest house hoping Devereux was home. I knew our magic put together would keep Dax out for sure.

"Devereux!" I cried as I entered his room.

"Xena!" V covered her naked body with a pillow. "I can explain."

"Don't bother. Consider yourselves fired." I stumbled out.

I could hear them calling after me as I stormed into the house. It took all of my strength to not give into the weakness that was building up in my knees. As soon as I was safe inside, I heard a car pulling up in the driveway. A few seconds later I could hear Isis' and Zoe's voices.

"Xena." Isis unlocked the door and walked in with the girls behind her.

"Isis." My body collapsed.

"Xena!" She ran over to me frantically.

"What do we do?" Zoe stood over me.

"Stay with me." Isis begged as their faces blurred.

"What happened?" Sarai pulled me into her lap.

"Guys." Her voice shook. "She's bleeding. A lot."

"We need to heal her." Isis instructed. "Let's get her upstairs."

My eyes forced closed and when I came to, I was in my bed.

"Look, I think she's waking up." Sarai's face became visible. "Xena?"

"Xena." Isis sat down next to me. "Please say you're okay."

"I – I'm okay." I cleared my throat. "What happened?"

"We had to heal you. You tell us." She grabbed my hand.

"I – I don't remember." I lied.

"Well?" Zoe and Sarai looked at Isis.

"She's lying." She nodded.

"You don't have to lie to us. We're your friends." Sarai assured me.

"Yeah, Let us be here for you." Zoe added. "Please."

"It was Dax." I admitted.

"Did he?" Isis asked infuriated.

"No." I shook my head.

"I will kill him." She avowed.

"He's not worth it." I talked her down.

"Or we could use our powers to charm him?" Zoe smiled deviously.

"Charm him into what?" Sarai smirked.

"Into loving Lisa." She shrugged.

"No, I hate Lisa but I would never wish this upon her." I refused.

"Fine." She contemplated. "What about a potion for him to unlove you? Is that possible?"

"We can try." Isis nodded.

"All you'd have to do is get it in his system. You could plan a pretend date or something." Zoe added.

"It's a good thing I always keep a travel pack with me. I got just what we need." Sarai winked.

"I'll help." I tried to climb out of bed.

"No, you stay right there." She pushed me back down. "We'll do all the work."

"Oh, but we're going to need this." Sarai replaced my bloody pillow with the dry one next to me.

They all formed a circle around the small cauldron Isis pulled from my closet and began chanting as the potion brewed. I watched as they filled two small vials with the green concoction.

"Perfect." Sarai smiled. "One for the shot, two for the kill."

"What?" I sat up.

"Not literally." She sighed. "Just saying, if you miss your first chance, here is your second."

"Oh." I smiled. "Thanks guys."

"What are friends for?" Isis winked.

VIII: OVERTURES

"Wake up!" Veronica pulled open my curtains.

"Get out." I groaned.

"It's time to get up. Your father said you are accompanying him to a brunch meeting in another dimension." She leaned against my dresser.

"Why are you still talking to me?" I put the pillow over my head.

"Because you aren't out of bed yet." She snatched it away.

"There. I'm out of bed. Now get out." I stood to my feet annoyed.

"Wow. You are really angry with me." She said frowning. "I-"

"Out!" I opened the door for her.

"Be ready by 10." She stormed out.

I slammed my door angrily to let her know that I was serious. How could someone that was supposed to protect me just leave me for dead like that? I am the reason she is here with a roof over her head and money in her pockets. I'm the reason she eats and sleeps comfortably. V and I had never had a fight before but I didn't care to cry about it. There was enough going on in my life. I didn't need the pressure of her regret weighing me down.

"Mother." I pressed the intercom button.

"Yes?" She answered.

"Casual or formal?" I sighed.

"Your royal blue dress has already been picked out for you." She informed me.

"Are you sure?" I asked, remembering how exposing it was.

"Yes, I'm sure. Your father agrees as well." She confirmed.

"Be down in a little." I said smiling.

I quickly pulled my hair into a relaxed updo and teased my eyes with mascara. I skipped over to my closet and I pulled the royal blue backless lace dress from its bag and pulled the black flats from the bottom along with the small black wallet. I didn't know if this was my father's way of making up to me but I was surely impressed.

I stepped in the dress and pulled it over my shoulders lightly.

The fabric tickled my body as it formed to my shape.

My appearance was professional yet cautiously casual. I threw the small purse over my shoulder, and walked out with my notepad in my hand. I knew wherever we were going I was bound to get bored listening to Fathers rambling. I decided I would write letters to Owen since that was the only thing that kept me smiling besides the brownies.

"You ready?" My father asked as I joined them in the portal room.

"Yes." I nodded.

"You look lovely." He complimented me.

"Thanks." I avoided eye contact.

"Go ahead." He gave my mother the signal.

She placed her hand against the scanner and the bright lights began to flash. As she pulled away the lights turned off and the door opened on its own.

"What dimension?" I asked as we stepped into an unfamiliar room.

"3rd." My father nodded. "We are at the Blacksfer Estate."

"The what?" My jaw dropped.

"I know what you're thinking." He stopped me.

"You do?" I looked down at my feet.

"You're thinking we are going to be attacked by vampires. But this is just business and trust me, Aldrin couldn't kill me if he wanted to." He smiled. "Now let's go."

"Aldrin." He stepped into the hallway.

"I'm here!" He shouted back. "I'm downstairs in the kitchen!"

Mother and I followed behind Father as he led us into the kitchen where Aldrin was standing at the island dicing tomatoes.

"We're having omelettes. I hope you don't mind." He smiled at us. "It's a self-serving bar for toppings."

He pointed to the table covered with trays of toppings and sauces.

"We don't mind at all. Do we family?" My father smiled.

"No." Mother and I said shyly.

"Hello Xena, Azura." He greeted us warmly.

"Hello." I smiled.

"One moment." He walked out of the kitchen. "Owen, Charlotte!"

"They'll be here in a moment." He promised.

"Okay." My mother nodded.

"Please have a seat. They shouldn't be long." He oiled the pan.

"I'll help." My father joined him at the stove.

I sat down at the empty table so nervous that I no longer had an appetite. This many coincidences I was starting to think it was fate.

"Would you like me to prepare your omelette?" My mother asked taking her seat across from me.

"No thank you." I smiled respectfully.

"Kids, say hello to the Briarwoods. Owen, you know Brice-"

"Brice?" I heard Owen's voice.

"Mrs. and Ms. Briarwood." He smiled looking slightly past us.

I'm sure my mother didn't notice but I did. It took me a moment to realize there was a girl standing next to him.

What was her name? Charlotte.

My eyes flashed back to Owen.

"Look at me." I repeated in my head.

"Hello." My mother smiled at both of them.

"Hello." Charlotte waved at us.

"I suggest you choose your toppings now." Aldrin smiled.

Everyone walked over to the bar two by two. First was Charlotte and Mother. Next was Owen and I. We walked awkwardly over to the table.

"I missed you." He poured black olives onto his plate.

"I missed you too." I picked through the unwanted toppings.

"Did you get my text?" I whispered.

"Oh, no. I don't like onions!" He spoke loud enough for everyone to assume that our conversation was just that innocent.

"Yes. Did you get mine?" He started putting random vegetables on our plates to buy us time.

"Xena." My mother called for me.

"What are you eating an omelette or a pizza?" I joked before joining Mother in the line at the stove.

Everyone was steps ahead of us while we stood back giving them space.

"Are you nervous?" He whispered.

"No. Why?" I whispered back.

"Your jaw tightens every time you get nervous." He said with a controlled smile.

"Does not." I argued.

"Point proven." He chuckled.

"Go away." I stepped up to receive my omelet.

"I like your dress." Charlotte complimented me as we all sat down at the table.

"Thank you. I like yours too." I smiled at her.

"Check it out." Owen sat down next to me trying to hide his smile.

His omelette was filled with so many toppings it was about to burst. I giggled at the sight.

"I'd like to bring up the first order of business." Aldrin announced.

"Which is?" My mother asked as she cut into her food.

"Brice and I are going into business together." He smiled.

"You are?" Owen and I asked at the same time.

"We are." My father nodded.

"Doing what?" Charlotte asked curiously.

"That is a surprise." Her father answered.

"But, we are going to partner up for the DCT also known as the dimensional convention tour." My father interjected.

"And when is that?" I chimed in.

"In about a week or two." Aldrin smiled.

"And you'll be gone for a week right?" Owen asked, swallowing down his last bite with juice.

"Yes. Just a week." He smiled.

"Actually, if everyone is done I would like to excuse the children from the table." Aldrin smiled.

"It was delicious." I complimented him as we all stood up in sync.

"Thank you Xena." He nodded at me. "Such a respectable daughter you have Brice."

"Thank you, I've raised her well." He took full credit.

I watched the quiver behind my mother's smile. She wasn't going to show her disappointment but I could see it. Maybe she was finally seeing in him what I always saw.

"Brunch was delicious as always Dad." Charlotte smiled before she dismissed herself.

"Xena, I will come find you when it is time to go." My father signaled it was okay for me to leave.

Owen and I walked side by side as we followed behind Charlotte.

"Finally." Owen sighed.

Charlotte sped around the house making it almost impossible for me to keep up.

"Charlotte!" He called after her.

"Yes?" She stopped at the top of the stairs.

"Xena isn't a vampire." He reminded her.

"Meaning?" She looked back at me.

"Meaning she can't keep up with you." He awkwardly stared at her.

"Oh right." She blushed. "Sorry, Xena. Be right back."

"It's okay, It was cool seeing you move so swiftly." I giggled.

"Let's go sit in the living room upstairs, It will be harder for him to listen in on our conversation if we are up there." He motioned for me to walk before him. As soon as the coast was clear, Owen grabbed me by my wrist and pulled me into the loft area. He moved my hair from my face and stared straight into my eyes. Slowly our faces began moving towards each other. His soft lips seemed to fit perfectly in mine, making my heart flutter uncontrollably. He was so gentle, yet so cautious. It was only a moment before he pulled away and left me standing alone.

"Charlotte's coming." He sat down on the couch. "Sit with me."

As I took my seat next to him, Charlotte walked into the room holding a fluffy orange cat.

"Xena meet Tizzy." She said joining us on the couch.

"How cute, can I hold her?" I asked as I stroked her fur.

"Of course." She placed Tizzy on my lap.

"I love cats." I smiled as Tizzy purred.

"I think she loves you too." Owen chuckled.

"She doesn't even like Owen." Charlotte laughed.

"She does too." He grabbed Tizzy from my lap. She screeched loudly and broke free from his grip sending her down the hallway.

"Tizzy!" Charlotte ran after her.

"Have I told you I missed you yet?" He brushed his fingers across my cheek.

"Would you like to see my room?" He kissed me.

"I'd love to." I nodded as he pulled me to my feet.

He guided me to his room and pushed the door open.

His walls were completely white and covered in black picture frames that complimented his headboard. I looked around his room smiling. It felt good to be here. It felt good to know he trusted me in his most sacred and personal space.

"I like your room." I smiled.

"Thank you." He watched me. "This is my old room though. I live with Rowan now."

"And your father let you keep your room?" I looked around.

"I know it's weird but he has a lot of work parties and I spend the night if they last too long." He sat on his bed.

"I don't think that's weird at all." I smirked. "So when do I get to see your other room?"

"Xena?" Charlotte said entering his room. "Your father wants you, I think you are returning home."

"Oh, okay." I simpered.

Charlotte and Owen walked me downstairs. I was hoping to be alone to say goodbye but Charlotte stayed by our side.

"Kids." Aldrin greeted us. "Xena, it was such a pleasure to have you, I hope we get to see you again in the near future."

"I hope so too." I glanced over at Owen and Charlotte.

"Brice, and the beautiful Azura." He led all three of us into his study.

"Call me." Aldrin said before closing the door.

"Will do." My father placed his hand on the scanner.

I stood there emotionless, already missing Owen as if I didn't just leave him. How was that possible? Would it ever be possible to want for another the way I wanted Owen?

We walked back into the house in silence. By the look on my father's face, he was content with the business deal he just made. Usually Mother and I would get an ear full on the way home when he was displeased but not this time.

"Xena." My mother started.

"I'll be in my room." I rushed upstairs before they could lecture me.

I didn't want to talk about what happened. I didn't even want to talk to my father. All I wanted was to be away from them. I plopped down in my bed and began to reminisce about this morning. It was perfect for the most part. I got to be with him and my father didn't suspect a thing. We were allowed to be friends and that was enough for me. My father usually never allowed me to leave his side during a meeting, but this time it was as if he wanted us to befriend one another. Maybe now that they're in business Owen and I will get a chance to be together more often.

I pulled the loose floorboard and grabbed the cell phone.

'Two unread messages' flashed across the screen sending butterflies to my throat.
"Hey it's me, I miss you more. I could get in so much trouble doing this but I don't care. When can I see you again?" I smiled goofily as I slid open the other message. *"Are you going to the games on Friday?"*

"If you promise to be there, I'll be there." I responded.

I could tell by the heaviness in the footsteps that grew louder and louder, that it was my father coming to talk to me. I placed the phone back under the floorboards, climbed into bed and pretended to be asleep.
As I waited for him I must've dozed off because when I opened my eyes the moonlight was shining onto my honey glazed floors.

"Xena, my office." My father's voice echoed over the intercom.

"What could he want now?" I whispered to myself as I rushed down the stairs.

I kept my steps light as I approached his office door.

"Come on in!" He shouted.

I slowly pushed the door open and stepped inside. Father was sitting at his desk rifling through paperwork that completely covered his desk.

"Hello Father." I stared at the new certification hanging on the wall behind him.

"What's that for?" I made conversation.

"Oh that?" He turned to admire it. "That is kind of what I wanted to talk to you about. Please, sit."

I cautiously took my seat across from him and waited for him to begin. Father always ran on his own time, if he knew you were waiting he would take even longer than he originally planned to. I sat there trying not to show on my face what I was feeling inside. I knew that would only give him ammunition.

"So, as you know Aldrin and I have been talking about going into business together." He started. "Well, it's been up and running for a while now, we just weren't ready to publicize it yet. But we are now!"

"I'm confused." I spoke truthfully.

"Xena." He sighed. "Aldrin and I have a company together and we want you to come work for us."

Would Owen be there?

"What? Don't look at me like that." He simpered. "I just think you would do well in the industry, that's all."

"What would I have to do?" I tried to hide my sudden interest.

"Just be in the office. Answering phones, dealing with clients who come in with BSD cases-"

"But-"

"Opening services for that is illegal, we know. That's why it's been under wraps for so long, but we are working on getting that overtured due to all of the victims." He said with a smirk. "It'll look really good on your college applications. The experience could even get you into better colleges-"

"What's better than MU?" I said with a hint of sarcasm.

"Human ones." He bribed me. "But only if you can handle the tasks."

He was trying to make me an offer I couldn't refuse.

"When would I start?" I gave in.

IX: BDSR

As we pulled up to the building oddly similar to the WGW, I couldn't help but reminisce. I sat in the back seat hiding my grin. This was definitely something my father had a hand in designing. I was certain that the chrome trimmings around the windows were his idea. He always added unnecessary touches to try and stand out but to me, it always seemed unoriginal and ordinary.

"Alright have a great first day, Honey." My father smiled as Thomas opened my car door.

"But-" I started.

"But nothing. It's your first day in the real world. I can't hold your hand everywhere, Xena." He said coldly looking out the window.

I said nothing and headed into the building.

"You'll do great, Honey!" He shouted in a monotone voice.

I walked through the revolving doors and over to the front desk. That was the only thing in the room. Everything else was blocked off by walls and doors making me anxious to discover what was behind them. I stood at the empty desk staring at the "BSD Revolution" sign behind it.

The sound of a door opening made my stomach drop. I turned to see a blonde woman approaching me with a clipboard in hand.

"Oh, hello." She smiled warmly. "You must be Xena."

"Yes." I nodded shyly.

"Welcome to BSDR, my name is Ember. Before I show you the ropes we should go over a few things." She handed me a folder full of paperwork. "Have all of those signed and returned by the end of your trial period."

"Trial period?" I looked down at the folder confused.

"Yes, just think of it as a probationary period. You have a few weeks to prove yourself worthy of your position before we replace you." She said with a hint of snide.

"Uh, okay." I nodded.

"Follow me." She sighed.

She led me through a door with a narrow hallway and over to the elevators.

She tapped her halo-badge against the small machine block beside the metal doors and they slid open.

As we stepped in, I saw a dozen offices on either side of us with a conference room in the center that divided them. The walls were made of glass, cutting off any form of privacy. All of the offices looked the same. Basic. A big desk with a computer and an office phone. The loud chatter from the offices filled my ears making it difficult to stay focused on Ember.

For the next hour, we toured the office. She showed me the areas I needed to know about and was more than eager to flee as soon as my back was turned. I met a handful of beings that I couldn't even remember the names of due to nervousness. Everyone was beyond professional, causing me to feel completely out of place. I was still a child compared to them. Completely inexperienced in this setting. I thought I was walking into a place full of amateurs, my father let me come in unprepared.

A loud blaring cut off my train of thoughts and forced me out of my seat. I stood there awkwardly as everyone walked into the conference room.

"Come on Xena." A small voice said as they entered the room.

I rushed in behind them hoping to blend in with the crowd.

"Good morning team!" Another tall blonde woman greeted us.

"Good morning Jen." Everyone chimed back eagerly.

I looked around at all the straight faces, so bleak to be as enthusiastic as they seemed.

"I'd like to introduce our new team member!" She shouted overdramatically. "Potentially, of course."

"To your feet Xena." She smiled.

Everyone greeted me warmly and I quickly returned to my seat.

"Now, onto important updates." She took her seat at the head of the table. "Does everyone, Xena exempt, have their updated blueprints and call sheets?"

"How could we not? You had our phones blaring at 5am with the holographic outlines." A brunette girl complained.

"That's because I know how you like your late night caps with Jason from the Lab." She hid her wicked smile.

"How did you—"

"Oh please, you really thought that was a secret? Everyone knows. He's been bragging about it for months." She scoffed.

"As you all know team week is approaching. We are getting double the calls so we need you working together. The owners will be in this week so really reflect on your team building skills. I will be watching. Even if I'm not around I have eyes watching you for me. You will be graded and possibly terminated depending on the outcome."

"Partners?" Someone groaned.

"Yes, partners." She sighed. "Problem Ryland?"

"Nothing that I care to mention, since I'm risking expulsion." He muttered.

"That's probably the smartest decision you've made in your entire career." She taunted him. "Now who wants the mute rookie as their partner?"

Everyone quickly became unavailable one by one. After Jen's snide comment I'm sure people were avoiding me intentionally. How could I blame them? No one would want to work with someone referred to as a *Mute Rookie*.

"Hey." A girl with sandy blonde hair stole the seat beside me.

"Hello." I flashed a smile.

"Don't worry about Jen, she's like that with everyone. Even her own mother can't stand her." She slid her glasses back up her face.

"Thank you." I smiled. "So, do you want to be partners?"

"Actually, I already have one." She smiled back.

"Oh, that's okay." I hid my embarrassment.

"But, he said you're more than welcome to join us." She grinned.

"Come on" She pulled me by my hand before I could even answer.

"Hello, Xena." He took my hand eagerly as we approached him. "I see Margo has retrieved a gift for Team Galactica."

"I thought we agreed on Team Ion." She argued.

"No. I shrugged at the suggestion. Big difference." He smirked.

"How about Ion Galactica?" I suggested.

"Awesome!" They both cheered.

"Now that everyone is partnered up and ready to go, let's start the call line." Jen spoke to the room. "While your call rooms are being set up, let's do a practice call to get everybody warmed up shall we?"

She looked around the room for who she wanted to victimize next.

"Xena" She smiled deviously. "Pick up the phone."

"Me?" I stopped breathing.

"Should I go back to referring to you as-"

"Not necessary." I cut her off and rushed over to the phone.

"Issac, can you plug in the red cord for me?" She asked with a hint of flirtation in her voice.

"Sure." He smiled.

"So what's my prompt?" I asked semi-confidently.

"Improv." She smirked.

"But-"

As soon as he plugged it in the line began to ring.

"What are you waiting for? Answer it!" She ordered.

"Hello, Thank you for calling BSD Revolution. This is-"

"Remain anonymous!" She quietly scolded me.

"One second please." I put them on hold.

"What the hell-" Jen started.

"I'm sorry. I need a prompt or something!" I panicked.

"No." She argued.

"What's with you?" Margo scolded her. "Here Xena, I have a cheat sheet. Just read 1-4."

"That might just cost you your promotion, Moreno." She threatened her.

I quickly skimmed the paper and resumed the call.

"Hello, sorry about that Ma'am. Thank you for calling BS Revolution, where we give you a solution. How may I help you?" I revised.

"Hello? My name is Miriam Zovirax. I'm calling from Arsenial Senior Housing. I'm calling because I believe my neighbor, Barbara Jones was murdered." As she spoke I searched through my bag to find a notepad and pen.

"What are you doing?" Jen whispered.

"It's going to be okay. What led you to believe something happened to her?" I ignored Jen and scribbled down the details.

"I hadn't heard from her in a few days, so I went over to check on her and I found her lying on the ground with a blue imprint in her neck. I rushed home to call the police but her body was gone when I returned." She explained.

"And did you contact them after you noticed?" I continued.

"Yes but, they told me that it was probably a night terror because they checked her home and it looked like she hadn't been home for a while. They said they found a note saying she went on vacation but I know her and I know she wouldn't go anywhere without me-"

"How could you possibly know that for sure?" I stopped her.

"Well, she is also my life partner." She revealed.

"I am *so* sorry." I empathized. "We will do the best we can to solve that for you. One second. I'm going to transfer you to one of our best agents. They will come out and assess shortly. Please hold."

Everyone cheered for me as Jen looked over in silence. I sat there feeling oddly proud of myself.

"That was awesome! We never get that much info out of a client before a transfer. She was just so comfortable with you. You're a natural." A girl complimented me. "It's Lindsay, by the way."

A wide smile spread across my face as I skimmed the pamphlet about our company. Maybe I could do this.

"I'll wait for the instructions, you guys go find our room and set up." Margo smiled.

"How will we know what room we're in without instructions?" Balic argued.

"She labeled them by team name." She informed him.

"But we didn't-"

"Yes, we did." She mumbled shamefully.

"Seriously?" He growled.

"Guys we don't have time for this. Let's go!" I pulled Balic out by his arm.

"Balic, I'm sorry!" She yelled after us.

"So, what are we looking for?" I asked as we turned down the hallway.

"Knowing Margo-" He trailed off as we searched through the doors.

"I knew it." He read the label on the door in disappointment. "After you."

I could tell Balic was really upset about the name switch. Margo was beyond assertive and so was he. I'm sure that's why they clashed so much.

I walked into the room in silence. The walls were so plain but the art beneath me took my breath away.

"Wow." I stared down at the beautiful mural under my feet.

"Oh, that. Every room has a different painting. It's our bosses way of being overly creative I guess." He shrugged as he drew on the whiteboard.

"Who Jen?" I scoffed.

"In her dreams." He chuckled and continued drawing. "Our boss is the real deal. He doesn't antagonize or embarrass you. He brings out your true potential and makes you see the world differently."

His hand moved so swiftly as his picture came together second by second.

"Now that's talent." I smirked. "How-"

All four phones began to ring, cutting off my stream of questions.

"Do we answer it?" I asked conflicted.

"Jen can kiss my ass until we get those instructions." He switched markers and began again.

I sat there for a moment contemplating if I should answer. The consequences seemed so slim after how well I handled the first call. If I was going to excel here, I needed to accelerate with confidence.

"I got it." I skipped over to the desk.

"Are you sure?" He looked back at me.

"Positive." I picked up the phone with confidence.

"Thank you for calling BS Revolution, how may I help you?" I smiled.

I put them on speaker so Balic could hear. The line was silent for a moment. I sat there patiently waiting for the caller to feel more comfortable.

"Hello." He finally spoke. "I'm calling to discuss the murder of my mother."

I recognized the voice immediately and froze.

"Hello?" Owen whispered. "Are you there?"

I couldn't. He would never forgive me for invading his privacy, especially if he wasn't ready to tell me. But, if I just hung up he would take it as a sign and it would make him give up on her case completely and I couldn't let him do that.

"Yes, I am here." I disguised my voice as best I could.

"How may we help you?" I looked up at Balic hoping it was buyable.

"Terrible." Balic shook his head and took his seat beside me.

"My name is-" He stopped himself. "Doesn't matter. I believe- No. I am certain that my mother was murdered. I am so tired of seeing case closed whenever I research her name. How could the case be closed if we never found her killer?"

"Can someone help me or not? I took a really big risk calling here." He angrily sobbed.

"I am so sorry to hear that." I held back my tears forgetting my disguise. "Let me-"

"Xena?" He sniffled. "Xena, is that you?"

I panicked and quickly detached the phone line.

"What did you just do?" Balic frowned.

"I got the instructions!" Margo cheered as she walked in.

Her smile faded as she quickly assessed that something was wrong.

"What happened?" She asked.

"I - I don't even know." I sighed.

"Well, for one thing, Xena is a terrible actress." Balic joked.

"I'm sure she's not that bad." Margo defended me with a smile.

As they continued their playful argument, I sat there regretting the moment I picked up that stupid phone. I should've waited with Margo or been stubborn like Balic. Now Owen will never forgive me.

"I gotta go." I sniffled as I stood to my feet.

"Xena, it's okay. Don't give up." Margo smiled.

"I just need some fresh air. Can you guys cover for me for a little?" I forced a smile.

"Anything for Team Ion Galactica." She placed her hand on my shoulder.

"Alright, break it up you two. We've got double the work to do now." He pulled Margo to the phones.

"Bye." I slipped out of the door.

I quickly took the side exit and rushed to the curbside. I pulled out my phone and called for Lars.

"I'll be right there Ms. Briarwood." He promised, and I knew he would be.

Father always had him parked around the corner just in case.

I stood by the curb blinking the tears away as they surfaced.

I couldn't let Lars know anything was wrong with me, he was my fathers eyes and ears for since before I was born. He loved to play the role of a distant parent, always watching and budding into the wrong situations.

I watched as the black SUV sped around the corner to my rescue. I took a deep breath and braced myself.

"Good afternoon Ms. Briarwood." Lars spoke as he opened the door for me. I climbed in the car and waited for his stream of questions to follow.

"So, how was your first day in the real world?" He smiled at me in the mirror.

"Fine." I flashed a fake smile and kept it short.

"It was that bad huh?" He continued.

"I said it was fine." I snarled.

"Message received." He turned the music up.

Lars always took things personally. That's one issue he and my father always revisit. He wears his emotions on his sleeve and Father liked to shove his under the rug. I didn't mind though, it was the easiest way for him to leave me alone.

I rode home in a comfortable silence with a loud mind.

The games were tomorrow and there was no way I would show my face there again. I was sure that Owen would tell Rowan, and the word would get back to Cat. That's already two founders and they have both lost their mothers. What if it rubs them the wrong way? How could I explain my side without offending them?

The knots tied in my stomach as we pulled up to my house.

"Your parents are inside waiting for you." Lars said as he snatched my door open. "I hope you're prepared to give them a better answer."

I climbed out of the car and rushed inside.

"Xena!" My mother greeted me at the door. "How was your first day?"

"Fine." I faked a smile.

"We need to talk, it's important." She smiled.

"Can it wait? I've had a long day." I slipped out of my shoes.

"Sure, but I-"

"Thanks." I rushed upstairs before she could change her mind.

The minute my head hit the pillow my emotions spilled through my eyelids. I knew I was better off focusing on school and never looking back at the games again.

X:INAUGURATE

"Xena." My mother rushed into my room, waking me out of my sleep. "Xena, wake up!"

"Isn't this Veronica's job?" I groaned as I sat up.

I could still feel the puffiness and soreness in my eyes. I sat there hoping she wouldn't notice.

"Normally yes, but your father has a surprise for you." She shrieked.

"Do I have to?" I sighed.

"You don't even know what it is yet." She sighed heavily. "Why aren't you ever happy?"

"I am, it's just-" I stopped. "What is it? What's the surprise?"

"I'll let your father tell you. He is downstairs eating breakfast. Hurry up and shower." I watched as she skimmed my room for flaws.

I climbed out of bed and awkwardly walked into the bathroom.

This was the complete opposite of what I was used to. Mother never woke me up or ever cared to share important news with me. That was Veronica's job, and even though I was upset, I missed her.

I stepped into the warm water and felt the nagging tension begin to melt away. What could Father want now? He'd already ruined my chance of getting into my dream college and now, because of his company, I lost Owen. If I didn't have anything to say to him before, I definitely didn't have anything to say now.

Most of my time spent in the shower was dedicated to my swarming thoughts of Owen. I needed to get him out of my head, even though a part of me didn't want to.

"Xena, it's been 15 minutes. Your fathers breakfast has probably digested by now." Mother said annoyed.

"Sorry." I turned the water off and reached for my robe.

"I picked out the perfect outfit for you." She said before leaving.

"Great." I mumbled.

I stared down at the hideous decision before me. She chose a lavender blazer with flowy pants. Mother could dress herself into a top model but couldn't dress me to save her life. Thank God I had Veronica and connections to the 1st dimension.

I decided on a compromise. I kept the blazer and grabbed my white dress from the closet. I quickly dropped my towel and slipped the dress over my body.

I spun in circles trying to get my zipper up.

"V." I sat down on my bed in defeat. "Where are you?"

My eyes locked on my wand and a grin spread across my face.

"Suclox!" The zipper quickly glided up my back.

I released my hair from its bun and walked over to my vanity.

I glanced up at my self-motivating notes on my mirror as I brushed the knots loose. I was used to accompanying my parents on every little boring trip they made but the need for me to get dressed before I knew where I was going was unsettling.

After applying light makeup, I searched for my shoes. The white heels with lavender trim complimented my outfit perfectly. I slipped them on and reached for the door.

Something told me to check the phone before I left. I quickly locked my door with a snap of my finger and pulled back the floorboard. I grabbed the phone and pressed unlock. I immediately clicked on messages.

"No new messages." Flashed across the phone.

Slightly wounded I put everything back in its place and walked out.

"Xena." My father greeted me at the bottom of the stairs.

"Father." I nodded once.

"Your outfit." He stared at me. "I think it's perfect for the occasion. Don't you, Honey?"

"What's the-"

"I do. I picked it out myself!" She cut me off.

"And beings say that your mother can't dress others." He chuckled. "Anyway, congrats Baby, you did it!"

He pulled me in for a hug.

"Did what?" I asked, feeling extremely awkward by his embrace.

"You got in!" He rushed to the front door and flung it open. "She got in! My daughter got into Marlsgate University!"

"Brice!" My mother scolded him. "The Briarwoods don't boast! Get inside."

"Sorry Dear." He walked back inside.

This was the first time I'd seen Mother remind him of anything morally good. She only cared about pleasing him, not helping him grow.

I got in. I didn't know how to feel but I definitely didn't want to go, especially not with human colleges now being an option.

I took a deep breath and plastered the biggest fake smile on my face.

"I got in!" I danced around.

"Thats right! And I've got an even bigger surprise for you." He slipped on his jacket and handed me mine.

"What's bigger than MU?" I tried to retain my enthusiasm.

"An interview with Witch Weekly. Veronica set it up for you when you first got accepted. They're waiting to hear from you. The beings want to know Xena Briarwood, this extraordinary young woman, Brice Briarwood's beloved daughter. Can you show them that?" He smiled.

"Of course. Let's go." I headed for the door.

As soon as I got outside two quick tears streamed down my face before I could catch them. My heart dropped when I saw Lars staring at me.

"Xena-"

"Not a word to my father. I mean it." I said as I climbed into the car.

I sat there waiting for Father and Lars to finish up their conversation. I usually didn't have the nerves to stand up to Lars so blatantly but he left me no choice. My father would only dig holes around the problem but he would never find it. He would never in a million years think he was the source of my unhappiness.

"This is it." My father slid into the passenger seat. "Are you excited?"

"Cant wait." I smiled back.

Lars got in the car and sped off. Their conversation drifted into his campaign in no time. I put in my charmed earphones and turned the volume down until silence surrounded me.

As we pulled into the driveway of the news station, my father got out of the car and left Lars with strict instructions on where to take me.

He wasted no time rushing to escort me in.

"Are you nervous?" He asked, breaking my preferred silence.

"A little." I nodded.

"That's way less than me." He pulled the door open for me.

"Thank you." I smiled as I walked into the studio.

The set up was similar to BSDR but this main lobby was packed with lobbyists and reporters.

"Welcome." A team greeted us at the door.

"Thank you for having me." I blushed.

"The pleasure is very much ours." He smiled. "Please, follow Rebekah to touch ups, she and Linda will prep you on your expectations and guidelines. Also, there is a recruiter from MU coming by to brief you."

Lars remained glued to my side as they walked me to my dressing room.

"Make yourself comfortable, we will be right back." They fled.

I stood there examining the room. The vanity was two times the size of mine and the view was beautiful. I could see all of Oxenfurt and for the first time I didn't feel so small. I could see all that I had to face and it seemed so minor now. I was just simply fearing the unknown.

"So why are *you* so nervous?" I turned to Lars.

"Truth be told, I always get that way whenever you get big news and new opportunities. It's been that way since you were a child." He confessed. "I guess I'm just really proud of you."

Before I could respond, Rebekah and Linda came rushing through the door with papers and cosmetics.

"Okay so, I'll be going over the guidelines for you." Linda approached me. "Sign this."

"And I'll be doing your touch ups." Rebekah guided me to the vanity chair.

"And I'll be briefing you." The door flew open.

"Zoru!" I exclaimed.

"Xena Briarwood." He grinned. "You made it."

"Of course, I wouldn't miss it for the world." I tried to smile over Rebekah's hand. "I didn't know you'd be here."

"Sign this too." Linda handed me a contract.

"A contract? For what exactly?" I asked confused. "A interview?"

"In this business, you have to sign a contract just to speak to someone important." She argued. "I'll be back with your final document."

"That's not what-"

"That's the real dimension for you." Rebekah chimed in. "Look kid, it's not to harm you, but to protect us. Beings come and go on tv acting all crazy and we lose profit. I can tell you're a nice girl so you have nothing to worry about just sign the papers. Besides, your makeup is done and so is this conversation." She exited the room.

"So, Xena." When I heard you were coming into the station to get interviewed I knew I had to be the one to brief you. It's only right." Zoru stole Linda's seat. "How are you?"

"Great." I smiled. "A little confused, but great and yourself?"

"Can't complain." He smiled. "You're used to the cameras and attention, aren't you?"

"Yeah, I've been around it my whole life." I sighed. "I'm very comfortable in front of the camera."

"That's great because this is about you. Your emotions on how it felt to get into MU. Your excitement. Your goals. Let us know more about Xena." He smiled.

"I can do that." I smiled back. "Definitely."

"Good. As long as you throw in good things about MU you should be good to go." He reached for me.

"Okay but where's my father?" I took his hand and stood to my feet.

"I have no idea. I was looking for him earlier myself." He frowned. "I'll go find him. Lars, can you escort her to set please? You remember where it is right?"

"Of course I do." Lars smirked.

"You know each other? College mates?" I asked as we walked into the elevator.

"And Brothers." He sighed as the doors opened in front of us.

It was hard to imagine their brotherhood when they came from two different worlds. Lars, the driver and confidant of the most important being in our dimension and Zoru, the MU recruiter with solid gold cufflinks.

"Welcome Xena." A woman rushed off the stage to meet me.

I could see the audience of happy beings waiting for us to begin. The cameras were set up in all angles, this was bigger than I thought. I was so happy I decided to alter Mothers outfit.

"Thank you for having me. You must be my interviewer." I reached for her hand.

"And Star News Anchor Angelique Sioux." She bragged.

"But who am I compared to *the* Xena Briarwood, daughter of the most nobel and sophisticated being of all dimensions?" She smirked.

"Just as amazing." I smiled back. "You know my Father?"

"Oh, isn't she cute?" She laughed obnoxiously. "Let's get started."

"You got this." Lars whispered as I was called to the stage.

"Wait Honey, here." My father stepped in front of me and shoved something in my ear.

"Ow." I groaned. "What is this?"

"Insurance." He gave me a push to go.

I took a deep breath and stepped onto the platform.

"Good morning Xena." Angelique greeted me.

"Ask how she is." My father's voice rang in my ear.

"Good morning Angelique. How are you this morning?" I forced a smile.

"I'm great. Let's jump right in shall we?" She grabbed her notecards. "Tell us about your dreams Xena."

"Well, I plan to start my own business one day. I-"

"No. You plan on taking over your fathers businesses. His dreams." He spoke, distracting me from my perfect answer.

"I mean." The mic squealed.

"My fathers business is still important to me. I plan to take over those as well." I combined the answers.

"That's very adult for a witch so young. Are you sure you want to take on all those *big* responsibilities? Are you sure you can handle it?" She challenged me.

"I know where I'm going." I answered confidently. "Do you?"

"Xena!" Father scolded me.

"Uh, well." She chuckled uncomfortably.

I could tell I put her on the spot. I waited for her to answer.

"I mean, look at me now. I'm a star news reporter." She bragged.

"Yes but is that the only accomplishment you wish to obtain in your career?" I challenged her.

"Of course not." She tried to hold her composure.

"Then me asking if you're ready for those responsibilities would seem a little insulting wouldn't it?" I smirked.

"I guess so." She drawled.

"Then please, do not assume I am not ready for mine." I smiled.

Smiles appeared across the faces of the crowd and I knew I made the right decision defending myself.

"Moving on." She cleared her throat. "Lets talk about MU."

"Mention me." Father hissed in my ear.

"Not only is MU my families alma mater, but my father also taught at that university. It would be a honor and a privilege to walk the halls they once did and take my place on the board one day." I lied.

"Amazing." She clapped with the crowd.

Seems like she bought the lies more than the truth. Either way didn't matter to me. I just wanted to get my father out of my ear and this interview out of the way.

"We can take a few questions from the live audience now." She gave them the floor.

Everyone raised their hands eagerly. I sat there choosing my poison.

"You with the nice glasses!" I pointed to the man waving his hands around.

"Perfect!" He exclaimed. "I've waited forever to meet you. My question is, is your father as controlling as sources say?"

"Uh, no. Of course not." I cleared my throat.

"Are you sure? Because my wife worked for the guy and he totally ripped her a new one for forgetting to clock out." He continued to pry.

"I-I don't know anything about that. Sorry." I shrugged uncomfortably. "Next question please?"

My father was strangely silent now.

"Hi yes, where do you get your attire?" A girl asked.

"Mostly from the 1st dimension." I nodded.

"You travel dimensions?" A judgy voice asked.

"Only with my parents of course." I smiled.

"We can take one more." Angelique encouraged the crowd.

"You." I pointed to a hand without a face.

The hooded person stood up to address me, keeping their face hidden.

"I heard that you reject people before even giving them a chance. Is that true?" The dark voice asked.

"Never." I answered confidently.

I always thought of myself as a good being. I reached my hand out all the time and I always strived to become better. Why was I being called out today?

"Liar!" The hoodie shouted. "You rejected me!"

I watched Angelique press the emergency security button.

Where was my Father?

"Who are you?" Angelique questioned wearily.

"Xena knows." He growled back. "Who am I Xena?"

"Dax?" I squinted past the bright lights.

"Bingo!" He stood up and revealed himself.

"Don't you come near her!" Lars lunged from the crowd and rushed towards him.

"Lars?" I stood up as the security guards pulled them both away.

"And that's all the time we have for questions." Angelique tried to regain control of the roaring crowd. "Xena, thank you for coming on. MU wants to offer you a paid trip to tour campus to get the real feel for the world you'll live in and to apologize for our crowd disturbance. Your father was supposed to pop in but I guess he got tied up. Thanks again. Xena Briarwood everyone!"

"Thanks for having me." I smiled and exited the stage.

As soon as I was sure the cameras couldn't see me anymore I began to panic. I saw Zoru standing at the dessert table.

"Okay, what the hell?" Angelique scolded the producers.

"Where's Lars?" I approached him.

"Xena." He smiled at me with frosting on his lip.

"Where is Lars?" I repeated sternly. "Where's my bodyguard?"

"I haven't seen him since they removed him." He shrugged.

"That was wrong by the way. He was only defending me. Wait until my father hears about this." I fumed.

"Your father saw the show going down and he fled as soon as he could. I doubt he'll be that infuriated." He spoke quietly. "Besides, you signed the contract. You have to retain the expectations you agreed to."

"Zoru, I want Lars and I want Lars now. I will cause a scene and have this entire set up shutdown. Don't make me ask again." I raised my voice enough to catch peoples attention.

"A girl who knows what they want at all costs. Can't deny that." He sighed.

"This way." He led me out of the studio and back into the hall. "He's right in there."

"Thank you." I rushed through the door to check on him. "Lars?"

"Xena!" He pulled the ice pack from his face exposing his black eye.

"Oh my god. Are you okay?" I hugged him.

I didn't realize my emotions until I expressed them. As bad as it sounds, I could treat Lars however *I* wanted to but the minute he was restrained everything in me told me to protect him. Maybe that's how Lars discovered his attachment to me. I get it now.

"I'm okay." He assured me. "Come on, let's get out of here."

He tossed the ice pack on the table and grabbed my hand.

"Where's Father?" I asked as we walked to the car.

"I haven't seen him, I'm sure he will turn up soon. Let's get you home." He said as he opened the door for me.

This car ride was different from any other.

Lars and I actually held a conversation without awkward silence swallowing it. I hadn't even noticed we pulled into the garage already.

"Thank you for being there for me." I smiled gratefully before climbing out of the car.

"Always." He promised.

I walked into the house and saw tables of food trays and champagne glasses all over the room. I continued into the archway to read the banner.

"Congratulations Xena." My father read it out behind me.

"Where were you?" I ignored his enthusiasm.

"I-"

Beings flooded through the front door, cutting off his response.

"Surprise Honey!" He cheered.

I stared at him in disappointment. I was sure he got all of these ideas from Veronica. These events had her name written all over it. He couldn't just take someone else's affection and wear it as his own. I was infuriated but willing to play nice once I saw my friends.

"Xena!" Isis rushed into my arms. "Guess what!"

"What?" I tried to seem as excited as she was.

"I got in too! We're going to college together!" She shrieked.

"No way." I grabbed her.

"Yes way. Look!" She pulled the envelope from her purse.

I could see the gold through the envelope and my shock transitioned into giddiness. Leaving this town would only be more perfect if Isis was with me and now she will be.

"I have so much to tell you." I pulled her away from the crowd.

"Wait for me!' Sarai followed.

I walked them into my study and locked the door.

"Tell us everything." Isis motioned me to come sit down.

"Don't leave out any details." Sarai added.

"Trust me, I won't." I sighed heavily.

I spent the next hour explaining everything that transpired in the last couple of days. There was so much I hadn't really processed until I said it out loud. Isis and Sarai were nothing but supportive of me. They asked questions and cared about the things no one else did. When I brought up Owen, my knees nearly gave out. It was strange being able to talk about him. Usually my feelings for him just stayed on a loop in my mind but I was unraveling it now and it felt good, like how it was supposed to feel. These girls were my family.

"That's deep X." Isis sympathized.

"Your dad's such a jerk." Sarai assured me. "He-"

Her sentence was cut off by knocking at the door.

"Who's that?" She whispered.

The knocking continued as I quietly unlocked the door. I took a step back and prepared myself.

"Come in!" I yelled as I picked up the baseball bat hiding behind the coat rack.

The knob jiggled and the door creaked open. I stood there with the bat raised and Isis behind me.

"Congratulations!" Zoe exclaimed.

"Zoe." I dropped the bat in relief. "I'm so sorry, I've been a little on edge lately."

"A little?" She joked. "Lydia was right behind me."

Before I could turn to look for her she was running towards me.

"Surprise!" She wrapped her arms around me. "And congrats!"

She placed a small red box in my hand.

"Thank you." I hugged her again in appreciation.

"Don't say I never helped you." She whispered in my ear.

"Hey guys!" She greeted our friends.

I walked into the hall and peered around the corner. The party seemed to be going well without me. I quickly rushed back into my study and locked the door.

"I just really wish I could see Owen y'know? So we could talk it out?" I sighed as I took my seat between Isis and Sarai.

"No offense X, but I highly doubt that." Sarai frowned.

"I know." My eyes watered.

"Good going." Isis thumped her.

"Wait, what did we miss?" Zoe complained. "You don't talk to him anymore?"

"You mean he doesnt talk to *me* anymore." I corrected her.

"But why?" Lydia frowned.

"I don't want to talk about it right now." I sighed.

"Well you can't just give up. That's not you." She defended me. "Let me think."

"Great. Asking Lyd to come up with a plan for you is like asking a baby to watch themselves." Zoe joked.

"No one asked you." She snapped. "Now be quiet and let me think."

"This'll take forever." Zoe whispered to Sarai.

"I have a way to cheer this party up." Isis stood to her feet and began searching through her bag.

"This is for tonight." She dangled the baggy of vials with purple potions in them.

"Is that what I think it is?" Zoe smirked.

"Pure. Straight from my Uncle's lab." She bragged.

"What's tonight?" I looked at them confused.

"That's it!" Lydia clapped. "I've got it! I know how to fix it!"

"How?" I questioned.

"The games." Everyone said in sync.

"Good plan Lyd." Sarai smiled.

"Told you I had it." She taunted Zoe.

"Good plan guys except you're forgetting one thing." I sat back down. "I have the leader of our dimension in my kitchen hosting my guests. I can't just leave. He'll get suspicious."

"Ask if you can sleep at my house." Isis suggested and everyone else agreed.

"I'm telling you guys, he wont let me." I said confidently, "But, since you don't believe me. Lets go ask him." I led them out of the door and back into the party.

Truth be told, as much as I wanted to see Owen, I wasn't ready to face him. I wasn't prepared to deal with the possibility of him never speaking to me again. Not to mention the fact that we would be trying to hash out personal problems at the games when we're not supposed to have any. It was just best that I stayed home. I was sure my father would deny my request anyway. This was the one time I wanted him to be - *him.*

"Father." I approached him.

"Xena" He sipped his glass. "What is it, Honey?"

"Can I please spend the night at Isis' tonight? She wants to have a spa party." I smiled.

I knew two things for certain, my father didn't care at all for cosmetics so he wouldn't see the importance of it and that it was my party. He wouldn't just let me leave. I stood there waiting for the answer I already knew.

"Well." He pondered as my heart sunk. "Sure Honey, it's your day. You did great at the interview and you earned me so many endorsements with that stunt."

"Stunt?" I growled. "The whole thing with Dax, that was you?"

"I did know about it, yes." He confessed. "Now nod and smile."

"No." I refused. "I can't believe you would do that. To me. To Lars."

"Xena, don't make a scene." He scolded me as he looked around.

"Please I-"

Thankfully his phone rang, cutting him off.

"Briarwood." He answered. "Aldrin?"

My stomach dropped to the floor when I realized it was Owen's dad.

"I'm on my way." He hung up. "Sorry honey, I'm going to have to go to the 2nd dimension. A crisis has come up. Just go to your party and leave the business details to the adults."

"Fine." I stormed off knowing my friends would follow.

I didn't stop walking until I reached Isis' car. I used my magic to teleport into her room. I sat there fuming, waiting for them to meet me.

"I guess she didn't need the keys." I heard Sarai say as they walked upstairs.

"Nope. Her magic works even when she's emotionally distraught." Isis said as she opened the door.

"We're so sorry, X." Lydia rubbed my shoulder.

"On the bright side, you get a night with your girls." Isis smiled.

XI: BEGUILED

"Are you sure this will make Owen notice me?" I said looking at myself in the bathroom mirror.

I was dressed head to toe in Isis' clothing. I was wearing a skin tight black dress with the highest heels I'd ever worn and my makeup was so drastic thanks to Sarai. I didn't feel like me at all, but maybe that was a good thing. Maybe that would help me fight the nerves.

"Definitely." Isis came out of the stall. "And if he won't, other boys will. You don't *need* him."

"I know, but I really want him." I sighed.

"But who needs boys when we have these?" Zoe dangled her vial.

"My turn." Sarai cheered and opened her mouth for Zoe.

I stood there feeling slightly uncomfortable as I watched them.

"Don't worry Xena, you won't die." Isis teased. "Just take two drops and wait for the ride."

"What does it feel like?" I asked skeptically.

"Indescribable. Stop with the questions and open up." Zoe walked towards me.

"Peer pressure much?" Lydia blocked her path.

"Oh hush, I'm just trying to get my best friend to relax." Zoe assured her.

"But not in a real way, not like a friend should." She continued. "You don't have to if you don't want to Xena."

"Enough." Sarai stopped them. "This isn't going to convince her of anything besides the fact that she has selfish ass friends."

"What the hell?" I read the poster on the wall.

"Why didn't you guys tell me this was a dance party? Is that why I'm dressed like I'm on the cover of something that Sarai's brothers read?" I ripped it down.

"It's true, I was inspired by page 65 of Dominatrix." Sarai smiled.

"Isis said you wouldn't come if you knew and we didn't want to risk it." Zoe confessed.

"She was right." I stormed out of the bathroom and into the middle of the Games introduction.

Because I'd heard it before, I felt comfortable enough to tune it out. I scanned the founders platform looking for Rowan. I knew that if he was here, Owen couldn't be too far behind him. I nervously waited for the host to finish.

"Hey!" Lydia clung to my side. "Sorry for what happened back there."

"You shouldn't be the one apologizing." I smiled at her. "What do you want to do?"

"I heard about this rescue course on the 5th floor." She nudged me.

"What do you have to do?" I sighed playfully.

"Easy. Boys get trapped inside a cage and the girls have to compete against each other to see who can rescue their damsel first." She explained.

"Talk about role reversal." I chuckled. "That's awesome. Who came up with this?"

"Catarina." She smiled.

"Of course she did." I smiled back. "She always looks for ways to humble those big headed boys."

"I know! She's so inspiring." She bubbled.

"Have you seen her tonight? I want to tell her something." I smirked.

"No, she's been M.I.A for a few games now." She frowned. "I was wondering why she didn't come to your party."

"Let's go to the 5th floor. Maybe she'll be there." I grabbed her hand.

"Are you going to do it?" She grinned. "Please do it."

"I was thinking about it." I admitted as we stepped into the elevator.

"I'm sure it would mean alot to Catarina to see her cousin kick ass at her own game." She smirked. "And who wouldn't want their name on the Hirou wall?"

Being on the Hirou wall was a big achievement. You receive a medal with a holographic memory of the moment along with your picture on the wall. All of the legends were on the Hirou wall including Catarina and her mother.

We entered the room and my eyes got big. The entire 5th floor was completely covered in a maze. I could see the cages for the boys at the end of it. They were raised high enough for them to see our every move as we raced to find them. The bleachers were practically hidbeings waiting to volunteer.

"You're going to kill it." Lydia encouraged me.

"You said two girls?" I asked for clarification.

"Well if it isn't little miss I'm not so perfect." A girl approached us.

"Do I know you?" I scoffed.

"Not at all but I know a lot about *you* since your little segment." She smirked.

"Chill out Elyza." Lydia defended me.

"Who is volunteering for the rescue course? You Xena? Or shall I say Nyomi?" She smirked. "That's right, I know your little secret."

"And what if I am?" I stepped closer to her.

"Then you'll be embarrassed, again. I win that challenge every time." She bragged. "I'm surprised your friends didn't tell you."

"They didn't need to tell me because I'm going to win. Watch me." I pulled Lydia over to the judge.

"I have a plan." She whispered. "Follow my lead."

"Hi, this is Nyomi. She is dying to volunteer, and since we know that Elyza is the competitor, is there any way you could skip the volunteer part and just go straight to the course?" She explained.

"No way. It's by random selection." He refused. "Fairly."

"Did I mention she is kin to Catarina Briarwood? She's practically royalty and she would love to compete." She folded her arms.

"Be ready to go on in five." He walked away.

"I can't believe that worked!" I hugged her.

"Never doubt the power of your best friend." She smiled. "Now let's go get you changed."

I followed her backstage and into a room filled with racks full of gear.

"Hurry. Put these on." She ripped Camo pants and a black tank top from the hanger and placed them in my arms along with some black combat boots.

"Nice pick." I complimented her style choice.

"Thanks! I saw what Elyza was going to wear. She won't even be able to run in that." She scoffed. "But you, you will be ready."

"So I'm just rescuing a boy from a tower basically?" I asked, trying to fight my nerves as I slipped my clothes on.

"Basically." She assured me. "You just have to find your way through the maze before she does and you win."

"Okay." I took a deep breath in and looked at myself in the mirror. "I can do this."

I pulled my hair up into a tight ponytail and laced my shoes.

"Nyomi." The announcer peeked in.

"Yes?" I turned to face him.

"Just wanted to give you a heads up that your partners have been chosen by the crowd. The boys will be waiting at the end of the maze for you. This is a competition. No matter what you do, do not forget that. And above all, have fun." He said before closing the door.

"See? Pretty simple right?" Lydia encouraged me.

"Yeah." I nodded doubtfully.

"90 seconds until the maze rescue begins!" The announcer roared over the speakers loudly.

"This is it." Lydia opened the door for me. "You got this!"

We walked out of the room and waited backstage for our names to be called. I could see Elyza hiding behind the curtain flirting with a crew member. She twirled her hair and giggled as he whispered in her ear. Her outfit was daring. She wore a black bodysuit that exposed her hips and boosted her cleavage. She was obviously looking for an advantage.

"Places everyone." The director whispered to us.

"Good luck." Elyza hissed as took her place beside me.

The curtains flew open and we were greeted by the anxious faces in the stands. The quiet murmurs from the crowd felt like loud critiques as nervousness set in. If she won every game, was I really prepared to lose in front of everyone?

"Competitors to your marks please." The announcer spoke. "Welcome to MazeGames, I'm Yodil Donovan and I have the pleasure of hosting this event with my beautiful Co-Star Melisma Pratt. Please allow us to introduce our brave new volunteer, who's kin to Catarina, Nyomi!"

The crowd cheered for me as I waved at them. My eyes locked on my five friends sitting in the first row to support me. I hid my smile as the announcer began again.

"And our undefeated champion, Elyza!" Melisma spoke more enthusiastically.

The crowd went wild in no time. Elyza walked around soaking up all the glory.

"We love you Elyza!" A girl shouted.

"But we can't forget about the main attraction." Melisma pointed to the cages.

The two boys were being lifted into the air with blindfolds on and no way out. I looked over at Elyza who was giving me the death stare now.

The crowd was beyond involved and entertained. They continued cheering as we waited to start.

"Let the games begin!" The announcers said in sync as the lights dimmed.

My anxiety piqued as Elyza and I were led down to the start of the maze.

"Now, there's no rules but one rule and what rule is that?" The announcer shouted to the crowd.

"No magic allowed and that's a fact!" They shouted back.

"That's right!" He laughed. "Witches, are you ready?"

"I am." Elyza rolled her eyes at me. "Are you?"

"Always." I smiled.

"That's what I like to hear!" He chuckled. "Ready the maze!"

The sound of the maze walls shifting made the crowd go wild again. I tried to focus beyond Elyza's singing.

"Can you keep it down?" I said annoyed.

"Why? Is it distracting you?" She smirked and continued.

"Go!" Rumbled throughout the room sending us speeding down our separate pathways.

The maze walls were so tall you couldn't see anything but the lights above you. I ran as fast as I could through the maze. I could hear the crowd cheering faintly as I met a dead end. I turned around to look for another way out as the walls began to shift again. I leaned against the wall and waited to see what was behind the opening one. This game was clearly about strategy. Something logical. Mechanical not magical. I watched the walls shift. I knew I was killing my time but it would be worth it if I was right. And I was. It was all about timing. After the last wall shifted, there was a clear path to the end of the maze. I smirked and headed for victory. I ran confidently until vines wrapped around my ankles and pulled me to the ground.

"Elyza!" I whispered as I untangled the vines.

As soon as I broke free, I heard hissing behind me. I slowly turned around to see a python slithering towards me. The walls had shifted and the view of the exit was gone. I ran as fast as I could to escape the snake, leading me deeper into the maze. When I turned around, he was gone and I was completely lost.

Feeling defeated, I finally gave in and used a spell to turn her feet into quicksand. I wanted to win fairly but she needed a taste of her own medicine. I didn't have time to go back to my previous strategy, I had to make it through before her. I pulled out my wand and kept it hidden at my side. I secretly moved the walls as I ran through the maze. As soon as I could see the end, I heard her struggling nearby. I laughed as I ran to the exit.

The crowd cheered as I rushed over to save my guy. I pushed the button on the wall and watched the cage until he was safely on the ground. I decided to show off and rescue her damsel too. I opened their cages and guided them out.

The crowd chanted my name until Elyza finally made it out. She said nothing as she walked over to shake my hand.

"Congrats Nyomi." She pulled me in close. "This isn't over, not by a long shot."

"Nyomi, please do the honor of unmasking your damsels and join us for your placement on the Hirou Wall!" The host shouted.

"With pleasure." I smirked.

The boys were standing there quietly conversing, waiting to be unmasked.

"May I?" I asked them.

They both nodded kindly.

I pulled the blindfold off of my guy first. It was only right. He smiled with a grateful grin and walked away. I proudly walked over to Elyza's damsel and unmasked him. My cockiness was quickly swallowed by panic.

"Owen." I gasped as butterflies and anxiety filled my chest.

"Nyomi." He answered awkwardly. "So, was it you?"

"Owen, there you are." Elyza walked up and grabbed his hand.

"I- I've gotta go." I handed him his blindfold and ran out.

I stormed into the bathroom and group texted my friends. I paced back and forth until they walked in.

"X." Isis rushed to my side.

"That was so embarrassing." I continued to pace.

"No, it wasn't." She grabbed my hands.

"No one even knew what was going on." Sarai reassured me.

"Owen did." I sighed.

"Look Xena, we're sorry for tricking you into coming. We just wanted you to have a good time." Isis hugged me.

"Really sorry." Sarai frowned. "Never again."

"Ever." Zoe joined our hug.

"You're forgiven." I sighed.

"Yay!" Isis cheered. "Now I can do this without feeling guilty."

She pulled out the purple vial and the girls huddled around her. I watched as Isis administered their drops.

"What does it feel like?" I asked skeptically.

"It feels like a super shot of adrenaline. Like the best dream you've ever had in HD." Isis smirked.

"It feels euphoric, like your entire body is being massaged." Sarai applied her lipstick.

"Everything's brighter, the world is better and the music." Zoe babbled. "The music is just-"

"I'll do it." I smiled.

"Don't feel pressured." Isis grabbed my hand.

"I don't feel pressured, I feel encouraged." I smirked. "I need to relax. Owen has my thoughts everywhere and I just need to silence the noise."

I opened my mouth and Isis poured a few drops in. I shivered as it hit the back of my throat. It was so bitter and not at all what I thought it would be.

"Let me know if you don't feel anything in an hour." She rubbed my back. "Ready to get out there?"

"Ready as I'll ever be." I sighed. "If I'm lucky, Owen has already left."

"Forget about Owen, let's go dance." Zoe grabbed me by the waist.

When we got to the 3rd floor, it was set up almost like a prom with DJ's and discoballs. Everyone was dancing and having a great time as I stood there awkwardly feeling out of place.

"My drops are kicking in, come dance with me." Isis guided me to the dance floor.

As we danced sensually, I slowly started to feel my body vibrating.

"You okay?" Isis pressed her lips to my ear.

I nodded as the music danced on my eardrums.

"Oh, someones feeling it." She giggled.

"Xena." Devereux pulled me away from Isis. "I know you hate me, I just wanted to come say goodbye. You have gotten into the college of your dreams and your father sees no use for me anymore. But you will always have a place in my heart, Xena. I left my contact information in your room if you ever need me." He walked away before I could respond.

When I turned around to find Isis, she was making out with Niko.

I discreetly scanned the crowd for Owen before shifting my eyes back to my feet.

"Looks like your date ditched you." Zoe looked over at Isis. "Let's get food."

We walked over to the table of food and Zoe started to stack slices of pizza onto her plate. I held back my laugh as I watched her.

"What? I get hungry when I'm floating." She chewed.

"Was it you?" Owen said behind me.

My palms began to sweat as I felt him standing over me.

"What?" I pretended not to hear him.

"Was that you on the phone yesterday?" He reiterated.

"No." I answered. "Well, maybe."

"How dare you? That was confidential!" He scolded me. "I wasn't ready for you to know yet!"

"What was I supposed to do? Just hang up on you?" I turned to face him with tears in my eyes. "I'm sorry, Owen."

"I gotta go." He picked up a plastic cup and blended into the crowd.

"What was that about?' Sarai rushed over to me.

"Oh nothing, I just ruin everything." I sighed.

"Why the sour faces?" Isis adjusted her dress as she walked up.

"Xena's sad." Zoe smacked on her food.

"Why? I saw Owen over here. You should be all smiles." She wiped the tears off my cheeks. "Do you need a boost?"

"A boost?" I sipped her cup.

"Yeah, another drop or two?" She nudged me.

"Hasn't she had enough? It's her first time." Sarai chimed in.

"Yeah but her emotions are high right now and she's a very powerful witch. It takes more to affect her. She's probably feeling the crash already." She explained. "Do you want more, X?"

"Sure." I nodded. "Let's go."

When we got back from the bathroom, Rowan pulled Isis away. As my high kicked in, so did my confidence. I made my way to the heart of the dance floor and locked eyes with Elyza, who was already watching me. I danced to the song as she burned a hole in the side of my face. As the beat picked up, I began to twirl and sway. More eyes were on me now and I secretly liked the attention. In the heat of the moment, I grabbed a guy from the crowd and pulled him in. He held my hips as I continued to dance and laugh.

"Xena." Owen stepped out of the crowd.

"What?" I continued to dance.

"Are you drunk?" He snarled.

"No. I haven't had a single drink." I spoke truthfully.

"Are- are you high?" He spoke through his teeth.

He pushed my dance partner away and stepped closer to me.

"Get away from me. You don't even like me." I sputtered.

"Of course I like you." He whispered.

"You said what?" I pretended I couldn't hear him although my knees were weak from his confession.

"Come with me." He tried to pull me away.

"Dance with me." I pulled him back.

"You're just intoxicated." He grimaced.

"I still want to dance with you." I spun around in front of him.

"Xena, we'll get in trouble." He muttered.

I continued to spin and feel the music. As light as I felt, I never felt more alive. I spun around until my body collapsed on the ground.

When I came to, I was in a room that I didn't recognize and my head was pounding so hard I could barely see. As I tried to refocus my eyes, I noticed the breathtaking view in front of me. There was a beautiful open patio with a sparkling infinity pool just beyond the glass doors.

"Where am I?" I whispered to myself.

"My house." Owen walked in with a breakfast tray.

"Your house? As in-"

"The 3rd dimension, yes." He nodded as he sat the tray next to me.

"My father is going to kill me. I have to get going." I tried to stand but my legs gave out.

"Easy." He rushed to my side. "You can't go home right now and neither can your father."

"What do you mean?" I asked nervously.

"Magic is down. You're stuck here and he's stuck in the 2nd dimension." He reiterated.

"And this girl refused to let you come without her." He flung his door open. "Rowan!"

Isis ran in and jumped on the bed.

"Thank God you're okay!" She kissed my face.

"Eat your food." Owen whispered before leaving to give us privacy.

"What happened?" I sipped the orange juice.

"Okay so, maybe I did overdose you a little bit." She winced.

"Oh, you think?" I rubbed my temples. "We're so screwed. What's our story?"

"We were at Sarai's. She'll cover for us." She nodded.

"That's actually kinda perfect. Better for my father to think that I was at Sarai's house with her house full of brothers than in another dimension with Owen." I ranted. "That could work."

"How do we get back?" She reached over and took a bite of my toast.

"I have no idea." I sighed.

"Sorry to interrupt ladies, I was just informed that magic is back up and running in your dimension, but still down in the 2nd. You'll make it back home before your father for sure." Owen smiled. "Marina set up a portal in the living room. You can go back home whenever you're ready."

"I'm ready! I gotta get home." Isis rushed to her feet. "Coming, X?"

I sat there contemplating my next move even though I already knew what I wanted to do. If I had an airtight alibi, why wouldn't I stay?

"Cover for me?" I smiled at Isis.

"Of course." She kissed my forehead. "Call when you get home?"

"I will." I nodded.

"You better take care of my best friend." She jeered.

"Will do." He smirked.

"So." I drawled with a smile.

"So." He chuckled. "Finish your breakfast and join me on the patio."

"Okay." I nodded shyly.

I looked down at my undesired spread of food and began to eat. I was unsure if he made it himself but I was impressed. The flavors were amazing but my stomach had other plans. I could feel the nausea rising but I finished it all for Owen's sake.

I placed my empty plates on the tray beside me and joined him on the patio.

He was standing by the pool, staring up at the bright sky.

"How was breakfast?" He looked over his shoulder.

"It was great. Who should I thank?" I smiled.

"That would be me." He turned to face me.

"Well, thank you." I nodded.

"I was wondering, can I talk to you?" He signaled me to sit down.

"Sure." I sat down awkwardly.

"I wanted to apologize to you. I'm sorry for snapping at you last night." He turned his back to me.

"It's alright, I barely remember it." I lied.

"Well I remember and I'm sorry." He sighed. "My mom's death has always been a sensitive subject for me."

"I get it." I spoke softly.

"Before I tell you the reason, can I ask why you answered that phone?" He looked at me over his shoulder.

"Yeah." I cleared my throat. "I work there, at BSDR. For my father and yours. I thought-"

"No. I knew of their dealings but I had no idea they were opening up an organization for-" He paused. "I had no idea."

"Yeah, my father has me interning there until college starts. I absolutely hate it there if that counts for anything." I walked over to him.

"I wish it did." He sighed.

"Owen, I think it's great what our fathers are doing. They're working to help those who have lost loved ones and potentially stop future killings." I assured him.

"It's just funny how my dad wants to help others but can't seem to help his own children suffering from the same thing." He chuckled dryly. "We need to heal, we need closure, we lost our Mom."

"Owen, I'm so sorry." I rubbed his back. "I had no idea."

"It's not something I advertise but yeah, my mother was murdered. Our family hasn't been the same since. My father doesn't even smile the same. When she died, it was like something in him broke." He explained.

"Same with my father when he lost my aunt. It's almost like he forgot how to love. He forgot that we still existed, that we still needed him." I fought the tears.

"I get it." He gently pulled me in front of him. "I really do. I'm here for you, Xi."

"Xi?" I met his eyes.

"Yeah, it's my little nickname. Cross between your two names." He smiled.

"I like it." I nodded bashfully.

"And I like you." He kissed me softly.

"And I like you too." I whispered. "I wish I could stay here."

"Lay with me?" He grabbed my hand.

"Of course." I smiled.

Butterflies swarmed around in my abdomen as he swept me off my feet.

I rested my head on his chest as he carried me into the house.

"Here you are." He softly laid me in bed.

"Not so fast." I locked my arms around his neck before he could pull away.

"Yes?" He hid his smile.

"I want you close." I stared into his eyes.

"How's this?" He pressed his body against mine.

"Closer." I whispered before kissing him.

When we kissed, nothing else mattered. He was my peace and something told me I was his. I didn't feel an ounce of guilt. All my thoughts were silenced. With him, I could live in the moment. As a rush of emotion filled my body, I began to explore his. His warm body with a cool touch gave my goosebumps the goosebumps. He ran his fingers through my hair and pulled it gently.

"Owen!" Rowan banged on the door.

"Not now, Bro!" He shouted back between kisses.

"Now is all we got. Xena needs to go home, now!" He bellowed.

Owen pulled away and sped to the door.

"What? What is it?" Owen walked out and slammed the door behind himself.

I laid there for what seemed like forever before gathering my things. Maybe Rowan wasn't as okay with this as I thought. Tears spilled over as I got ready.

"Xena." Owen walked in as I was slipping on my shoes.

"Yes?" I wiped my cheeks before I looked at him.

"Why are you crying?" He rushed to my side.

"It's nothing." I smiled. "What did Rowan say?"

"He said you have to go." He sighed.

"I knew it. He doesn't like me, does he?" I sniffled.

"Oh no, no. It's not that." He grabbed my face. "Magic is having some sort of malfunction and he wants to get you home before you get stuck here."

"You're sure that's the only reason?" I asked as we locked arms.

"I promise you." He kissed my forehead. "Lets get you home."

When we walked into the living room, Rowan was lounging on the couch, eating chips. I stood behind Owen awkwardly.

"Thanks for having me." I spoke shyly.

"Anytime Nyomi." He smiled.

"Our transportation room is right through there, Xi." Owen pointed to the green door. "It should take you right home."

"Right." I sighed as I turned to face him.

"I'll miss you." He stole a kiss.

"I'll miss you more." I fought my tears.

"I'll be seeing you soon." He opened the door for me.

"I hope so." I sighed as I stepped into the room.

"Take this." He handed me his flannel. "When you miss me the most, wear it."

"I will." I nodded.

"And then imagine me taking it off of you." He said before closing the door.

My cheeks ran hot as the light blue beams flashed around me. As soon as they turned white, I opened the door and walked into my dark hallway.

I sighed heavily as reality set in. As I crept up the steps, my mother walked through the door.

"Xena Nyomi Briarwood!" She slammed her purse down. "Where have you been?"

"Can we have this fight later, Mother? I'm really tired." I sighed.

"Tired?" She questioned me. "At 11 A.M? Where have you been?"

"I was with Sarai! Where were you?" I crossed my arms.

"I can smell the lies on you from here." She snarled. "You've changed."

"You're right, Mother. I have. Maybe you need to try it." I challenged her.

"You know what-"

"Girls." My father walked in. "What's going on?"

"And it gets better." I mumbled sarcastically. "I'm going to my room."

"Not before you answer me. Where were you?" My father approached me. "I got word that kids were sneaking out of our dimension and you weren't accounted for."

"I was with Isis. Why?" I sighed.

"I thought you said you were with Sarai-"

"And Isis, Mother." I rolled my eyes.

"I don't know." My father pondered. "You were acting strange at the party. Not like yourself."

"Why are you guys interrogating me? I'm fine!" I yelled.

"Do not shout at your father!" She yelled back.

"Oh please Mother, I hear you two almost every night." I chided. "I cannot wait to go to college!"

"That's it, young lady! I don't know what's gotten into you but I don't like it. You're going to be spending a lot more time at work and home with your family and less time with your delinquent little friends." She ordered.

"Home? You're never even here! Just send me to my room now. I have nothing else to say." I shut down.

My mother stormed away mumbling to herself while Father stood there with an unreadable look on his face. *What was he thinking?*

"Work tomorrow. Be there." He dismissed me.

I gladly stormed up the stairs and into my room. I quickly pulled my cell phone from my purse and called Isis.

"Hello?" She whispered.

"Who got caught?" I whispered back.

"I don't know, it wasn't me. I was safe in my bed when my parents got the alarm." She bragged.

"I wish you would've tipped me off Isis. My parents are the absolute worst." I plopped down on my bed.

"We can run away." She said sincerely.

"I wish but I really need this internship if I want a real chance of getting out of here." I sighed.

"I wish I could work there with you." She whined.

"Ask your Godfather. I'm sure he wouldn't mind." I suggested. "Have you talked to Sarai?"

"Not since the games. The last conversation we had she said she would cover for us. I'm going to add her to the call, one second." She clicked over.

I sat there waiting for her return. My thoughts quickly drifted to Owen.

"No answer." Isis huffed.

"That's weird." I kicked off my shoes. "Her phone is always glued to her side."

"I'm worried-"

"Xena!" My mother shouted.

"Gotta go." I hung up the phone and pretended to be asleep.

I could hear her heels traveling down the hallway. My door creaked open and I laid there as still as possible until I heard it close.

XII: KVETCHING

The next few days were almost unbearable, work was unfulfilling. I tried my hardest to avoid my parents and I felt like at some point, they were doing the same. I didn't mind. I wanted to be alone. I needed to be alone. Isis and Sarai were radio silent, Owen hadn't messaged me back. I was just as alone as I felt. Today we had a dimensional meeting. They were rare but always serious. As I got ready, my nerves began to go haywire. Did the council find out about the games? Did something happen to a founder? I'd never gotten ready so fast in my life. I was already waiting in the car by the time my parents came down for breakfast.

We rode in silence for the most part, minus the small talk between Lars and I. He was the only being that I actually enjoyed talking to. I was ready to fully forgive Veronica, if only she would come back. I had no idea where she was and my parents' loved the fact that I was missing her.

We walked into the building and everyone was waiting quietly in their seats. It was like they were waiting for us to arrive. I awkwardly walked behind my parents as they headed to the stage. My father guided me to the first row and continued to the podium. My eyes locked on Sarai who was sitting with her brothers. She looked so sad. A sick feeling grew in my stomach as my father started to speak.

"Hello beloved beings of Oxenfurt." He started. "I'm sure some of you know what has happened this week. Tragedy has struck yet again. It's with a sad heart that I have to announce that we have lost another amazing, courageous being to BSD."

My heart dropped to the floor as I pieced together what had happened. I looked back over at Sarai who was sobbing uncontrollably. I fought the tears as her mother entered the room. You could feel her pain as she made way over to her children. She was broken. They all were. I scanned the room for Isis but she wasn't here.

"Now is the time to buckle down and take things more seriously. I am going to implement a curfew starting tonight. 8pm. The only exception is work duty and you would need to provide proof. All beings under the age of 18 must be accompanied by an adult after curfew. If we catch you out, you will be punished accordingly." He spoke sternly. "And now, we would like to take a few moments to pay tribute to our fallen, Raul Orozco. My wife will now come up and speak on behalf of his family and our community."

He stepped down and guided my mother to the microphone. She cleared her throat before she spoke.

"Hello all." She sniffled. "I want to start by saying-"

"No!" Jenna, Sarai's mother shouted.

Everyone watched silently as she rushed to the stage.

"I'm sorry Azura, I just don't feel right letting someone else speak for our loss." She sputtered.

"No. I completely understand." Mother rubbed her back. "The floor is yours."

"Thanks." She stepped in front of her and adjusted the microphone.

"Family." She started. "That is what we all are. This community. We are a family. When one loses, we all lose. I know many of you loved Raul and he loved all of you. He always found ways to give back, even to the beings outside of Oxenfurt, even though it was frowned upon. He was fearless, he was a provider."

As her voice broke, many beings in the crowd started to cry. I wanted to so badly to run over there and console Sarai but I knew it wasn't the time. I swallowed my emotions and tuned back into her mothers speech.

"To my babies, Lo siento. I cannot express how sorry I am. I wish I could bring your papa back. I would give anything to bring him back! We will get through this. I promise. He is still with us, he is here now. Para siempre." She spoke through her tears. "And to whoever did this, whoever took him from us, you will be found out. We will have justice. One way or another. You can't hide in the shadows for long."

She stepped down and rejoined her family who welcomed her with hugs.

"Thank you, Jenna. What a powerful message." My father clapped for her.

Everyone clapped along until my father stopped.

"That concludes the end of this meeting. Remember the curfew." He waved. "Have a good day."

As soon as he dismissed us, I saw Isis walk out from the backroom with her parents. She walked over to me with tears in her eyes.

"X." She reached for me.

"Where were you?" I hugged her.

"I'm sorry, I couldn't watch that." She cried.

"No, I get it." I wiped her tears. "Lets go console Sarai, she needs us."

"Okay." She sniffled.

We walked over to her hand in hand. I swallowed hard before speaking.

"Sarai." I tapped her on the shoulder.

She turned around with puffy eyes and a broken heart.

"Hi." She simpered.

"We are *so* sorry." I sobbed.

"Where were you guys?" She pulled us away from everyone.

"What do you mean?" Isis whispered.

"While you two were out hooking up with boys from another dimension, my father was being murdered." She sputtered.

"Sarai-"

"Some friends you are." She stormed off.

Isis started to go after her but I pulled her back.

"Lets just give her space. She needs her family right now." I assured her.

"Fine." She sighed.

"Xena, we're leaving!" My father bellowed.

"Come over later?" I hugged Isis.

"I will. We need to talk." She whispered in my ear before she walked away.

I followed my parents out the door and into the car. The silence resumed the minute we sped off. Before Lars could park at home, I stormed into the house. I didn't want to be around them longer than I had to.

"Xena, wait!" My mother stopped me before I could get up the stairs.

"Not now." I looked back at her. "Today was enough. Can I mourn?"

"Of course, but I need to talk to you first." She slipped off her shoes.

"So, I can't." I sat down on the stairs. "What's up?"

"So, I'm looking into adopting a little Briarwood." She shrieked.

"You're what?" I crossed my arms.

"I said-"

"I heard what you said, why?" I dropped my purse at my feet.

"Well, because-"

"Why? Because you're doing so well with raising me? Or do you want Veronica to raise this one too?" I scoffed.

"I clearly went wrong with you Xena, I don't know where but I did. I want to do it right this time. A second chance, you know?" She frowned.

"Wrong Mother. You don't get to just hit reset as if you didn't neglect me my entire life. You don't get to bring in another innocent child to test the theory of you miraculously becoming a better parent overnight. You look me dead in my eyes, you see how unhappy I am, and nothing in you what's to fix that. Your maternal instincts are nonexistent." I sobbed.

"I'm sorry you feel that way but my mind is made up." She walked away and left me crying.

I stormed into my room and threw my purse against the wall in frustration. My blood was boiling. I couldn't wrap my head around her logic. She didn't need another child. She doesn't even need me. I pulled a bag from under my bed and filled it with clothes.

My phone vibrating loudly stopped me from gathering the rest of my things. It was Sarai.

"Hello?" I answered breathlessly.

"Xena, I'm sorry." She cried. "I didn't mean to snap on you like that. I know you would've been there if you could've."

"I'm sorry too. I wish I was." I sat down on my bed.

"You know they think I did it?" She whispered.

"Who? Who thinks that?" I whispered back.

"I gotta go. I love you." The line went dead.

How could they think Sarai was at all involved? She was the sweetest being and loved her Dad. She could never hurt him. She could never hurt anyone.

My heart ached for her as I finished packing. I couldn't help but cry.

"Xena, dinner!" My father shouted.

I wiped my tears and dropped my bag by the door as I walked out.

"Thank you for joining us." My mother greeted me.

"Yes, thank you." My father added.

"I know meals haven't been the same since Veronica-"

"Speaking of, when is she coming back?" I cut her off.

"Not sure. She had personal things to handle in the human dimension." She shrugged.

"Without saying goodbye?" I muttered.

"I guess your stand-in mother isn't as perfect after all." She smirked as she sipped her wine.

"Yes she is." I defended her.

"Enough." My father scolded us.

"Sorry Honey." She frowned.

"Xena, eat. We have a lot to discuss." My father ordered.

"Don't we always?" I sighed. "Can't we just have dinner? Today was a lot."

"It was." He nodded. "However, that doesn't change anything."

"Then go ahead." I put my fork down. "I'm not hungry anyway."

"I heard a rumor about different dimensions meeting up, do you have idea what that's about?" He tried to ask casually.

"No." I lied.

"So, that night we were gone, the next morning when we caught you coming home-"

"You didn't catch me doing anything. I was just coming home." I corrected him.

"Same thing." He chewed.

"Not really." I shrugged. "But what are you asking me?"

"Where were you? If you really were with Sarai like you say, did you see anything?" He looked over at my mother.

"No." I sipped my drink. "Because Sarai didn't do anything and neither did I."

I texted Isis under the table, knowing I was about to make my exit.

"But he died in the home, if you were there you must've seen something, heard something." He pried.

"Funny, you were unaccounted for too. Did you have anything to do with it?" I stormed off.

"Xena! You get back here!" He shouted.

I walked into my room and locked the door behind me. I grabbed my hidden phone and put it at the bottom of my bag. I climbed out the window and used the handhelds to get down.

When I got to Isis' door, she was standing there waiting for me.

"Welcome home." She smiled.

"Thank you." I hugged her as I walked in.

I spent the next few nights at Isis' house, and for the most part my parents were okay with it. They cared too much about their image to come and drag me out kicking and screaming. I loved being at Isis' house. There were no rules, no dress codes, just a normal household. Something that I feel I deserved to be a part of.

I stared out the window, watching the leaves fall. I couldn't figure out exactly how I felt but I was numb. I was tired. I didn't have any desire to go back home. I just wanted to get as far away from here as I could but I knew I was stuck next door to my nightmares. I was trapped.

"So, what are we doing today?" Isis walked in with breakfast.

"Wallowing." I sighed as I grabbed my plate. "Thank you."

"Absolutely not." She sat down in front of me.

"Then what?" I chewed.

"Shopping? Go check on Sarai?" She suggested.

"We can't. Her house is a literal crime scene, she can't even be there." I reminded her. "Besides, I think she's going back in for questioning today."

"She didn't do it." She barked.

"I know that." I sighed. "Convincing the council is the problem."

My duffle bag began to vibrate loudly and I pretended I didn't hear it. I trusted Isis with my life but the less she knew the better.

"So-"

"You're really going to pretend like your bag isn't ringing right next to me?" She crossed her arms.

"Huh?" I smiled.

"Huh." She mocked me.

She picked up my bag and searched until she found Catarina's phone.

"Whats this?" She waved it around. "You have a secret phone?"

"Technically it's Cats' secret phone." I rolled my eyes.

"You're sneakier than I thought, Babe." She unlocked the phone.

"Can you not?" I rushed over to her.

"I just want to see what else you've been hiding." She grinned.

"Nothing really." I reached for the phone.

"Owen called." She winked. "That's why you have this phone? To talk to your boyfriend?"

"He's not my-"

"I'm proud." She cut me off. "Let's call him back."

"Lets not." I snatched the phone.

"You're no fun." She plopped down on her bed. "I'll just call Rowan from mine and tell him how much you love and miss-"

"You wouldn't dare!" I growled.

"Watch me." She picked up her phone.

I chased her around the room until Isis' Mom barged in. We quickly sat down and hid the phone.

"Your Father is on a conference call!" She quietly scolded us.

"Sorry Mom." Isis frowned. "We were just playing around."

"At least wait until your Father leaves. I'll be downstairs prepping dinner." She smiled.

"Whats for dinner, Mom?" Isis made conversation.

"Beef stew and sweet bread." She kissed our heads before leaving.

"Call him back." She handed me the phone.

"Fine." I sighed.

"On speaker." She ordered.

Butterflies filled my stomach as I waited for him to pick up.

"Xi?" He whispered.

"Yeah, it's me." I cleared my throat.

"How are you?" He answered quickly.

"I'm okay." I sighed.

"I missed you, I just needed to hear your voice." He avowed.

"I missed you too." I turned away from Isis.

"I don't know if you've heard but the games have been canceled-"

"What?" Isis snatched the phone. "What do you mean canceled?"

"Yeah, Rowan just told me. He said some being got tipped off and we have to lay low for a while."

"Where is he? Is he around you?" She walked into the bathroom and closed the door.

I tried my hardest to listen but it was useless. My phone chimed in my back pocket and I immediately knew who it was. She had a specific text tone and I'd been waiting to hear from her for what felt like forever.

I'm back. Your parents said you left. Please come back home, I came back for you.

I quickly gathered my things and waited for Isis' return. There was nothing that could stop me from seeing Veronica. I needed to.

I laid back on the bed and drifted off.

"You're leaving?" Isis scared me awake.

"Sorry." She sat down next to me. "Why are you leaving?"

"Vero's back." I sat up rubbing my eyes.

"That's so exciting!" She exclaimed. "Are you going to come back?"

"I'll definitely try to." I nodded.

"Please?" She grabbed my hands. "I don't want you to have to deal with all that back home. I know you're right next door but at least you can relax here. I hate seeing you stressed like this. It kills me."

"I'm okay." I assured her.

"No. You're not." She pulled me close. "And that's okay."

I tried my hardest not to cry as she held me. There was something about Isis' embrace. Her energy was so nurturing. She was definitely the mom of our group.

"I'll come back. Don't worry." I kissed her forehead as I stood up.

She walked me downstairs with a frown on her face. I didn't want to leave her either but I had to. I had to talk to Veronica and see where she's been.

"What did Owen say?" I asked as we walked outside.

"Oh, he said-"

"Bunny!" Her father shouted.

"I'll tell you later." She kissed my cheek and fled.

When I got to my doorstep, regret instantly filled my body. Something in me told me to turn around but of course I ignored it.

As soon as I walked in, Veronica stole me away and dragged me into her room. She quietly closed her door and turned around to face me. I felt like I hadn't seen her in years. She was more beautiful than when she left. She was glowing and she looked so happy, despite the worried look on her face.

"Xena!" She embraced me.

"Hi." I sobbed.

"I missed you so much." She kissed my cheek.

"I missed you more." I sniffled.

"Wait. Let me look at you." She pried my arms from around her. "You are so beautiful."

"So are you." I wiped my tears. "Where have you been?"

She pulled me over to the bed and sat me down.

"You can keep a secret right?" She searched for the truth in my eyes.

"Of course I can." I nodded.

"I mean it. If anyone finds out about this, you will never be allowed to see me again." She warned me.

"You can trust me." I promised.

"I've been with Dev." She confessed.

"You have?" I smirked.

"Yes. I told your parents I had business to handle in my dimension but that wasn't true." She sighed. "I've been with Dev and we are so, so, happy, Xena."

"And I'm happy for you." I said sincerely.

"Really?" Her eyes lit up.

"Really I am. And I'm sorry for overreacting-"

"You have absolutely nothing to be sorry for." She hugged me. "That was our mistake, not yours."

"I just missed you so much." I fought my tears.

"Theres something else." She began to pace back and forth.

"What? What is it?" I watched her.

She unzipped her coat and exposed her round little belly.

"You're-"

"Shhh!" She rushed over to me. "You can't say a word."

I sat there silently, processing all of her secrets. I didn't want to overwhelm her with questions but I had so many.

"We didn't plan this. No one was ready for this." She started pacing again. "If your parents found out, I would never see you again. I almost didn't come back. Dev said it was too risky but I couldn't leave you like that. There was no way. I love you way too much. But I can't say that I'll stay forever. I mean how can I? I'm-"

"I know but how are you that far along? It hasn't been that long-"

"Time moves differently in his dimension." She shrugged.

"Hey. I need you to sit down, okay?" I reached for her. "If they hear you pacing around like that, you'll be caught anyway."

"Right." She rejoined me on the bed. "What do we do?"

"Stay in big coats, loose dresses, wear as many layers as their dress code permits until we figure out a solid plan. Stay in the shadows. If they don't need you, you are not seen." I coached her. "Are there any plans for tonight?"

"Yes. Plans that you may not like." She bit her lip. "Dax and his family are here for a few days. Something about a convention. I didn't get the details but I was trying to while I was preparing lunch."

"Great." I groaned.

"Warning, they seem especially pretentious since they were awarded all of that new land." She sighed.

"I'm sure." I rolled my eyes.

"I have to go prep dinner. Want to help?" She smiled.

"Yes." I stood up and pulled her to her feet. "The less work you have to do the better."

"Thank you." She zipped her coat and stepped into her shoes.

"Who knew you'd get knocked up by a fairy?" I teased as we walked out.

"Knocked up?" She chuckled. "Stay out of my movie stash."

When we got downstairs, I braced myself for my parents' punishment. We walked into the kitchen and found a note saying that they went out with Dax's parents and they would be back at midnight.

"Yeah, they're gone." Dax appeared in the doorway.

"I read that." I nodded sarcastically.

"Nice to see you too, Xena." He winked before walking back outside.

"Isn't he charming?" Veronica rolled her eyes.

The perfect plan popped in my head and I rushed upstairs to act on it.

I searched my drawers until I found the answer to my current problem.

"V, can you do me a favor?" I spoke through the intercom.

"Anything." She answered.

I instructed her to slide a note under Dax's door that said I wanted to have dinner with him at 9 and to prepare the most delicious meal. Something his family has requested before. I borrowed the most stunning red dress from Veronicas' closet. It was short and revealing. I knew he would be eating out of my hands just to see me in it.

"Xena, your guest is ready." Veronica's voice echoed up the stairs.

"Coming!" I shouted back.

I sprayed my favorite perfume and teased my cheeks with a little blush. I knew exactly how to play this.

"Wow." Dax smirked as I joined him.

Veronica had a separate table set up in the living room. It was small, intimate. There was a beautiful wicker candle burning between us. It definitely set the mood.

"You look stunning." He stared at me.

"Thank you." I nodded once.

"Hello." Veronica walked in with two plates of steak and lobster.

"Thanks V." I smiled up at her.

"Of course. Enjoy." She walked away.

"All of this for me?" He grinned.

"Yup. All of it." I cut into my food.

"I was wondering when you were going to come to your senses." He sipped his water. "We make the most sense, Xena."

"We do make sense don't we?" I forced a smile.

"Of course we do." He scoffed.

"I'll be back, I'm going to go get our champagne." I excused myself.

"Just a minute." He pulled me onto his lap. "You look too good walking past me."

"Well, thank you." I struggled to hide my discomfort.

"Kiss me." He pulled me in.

"Not before the champagne. I'm no cheap date." I flirted as I walked away.

"I like this new Xena!" He shouted after me.

I rushed over to the champagne glasses and emptied the potion into his. I swirled it around and walked back in with our glasses.

"I'm back." I handed him his glass and sat down.

"You know, I love champagne almost as much as I love you in that dress." He sipped his glass.

"We have to toast." I stopped him.

"To us." He held up his glass.

"To you." I smiled.

"I like that." He smiled back arrogantly. "To me."

"I'll be right back, I have to go to the bathroom. If you want more champagne its in the kitchen. Help yourself." I sipped my glass before walking out.

I walked into the bathroom and locked the door behind myself. I stared at myself in the mirror and thought back to all the times Dax pissed me off. The day of the interview was the worst. I stood there feeling justified in my decision. After all, it was just a potion to kill his attraction for me.

I gathered my thoughts and walked back into the living room.

"Dax?" I looked around.

I figured he was in the kitchen getting another glass and headed in there. When I walked in, Dax was lying on the floor with his eyes closed.

"Dax!" I rushed over to him.

"Dax, this isn't funny." I tried to shake him awake. "Wake up."

His body was limp and his skin was cool to touch. I knew he wasn't faking. I looked up at his empty glass on the counter.

"What did I do?" I whispered. "I'm going to go get some help."

I rushed upstairs and into Veronica's room.

"Xena, what is it?" She asked startled.

"It's Dax." I said breathlessly.

"What about him? Has he hurt you?" She grabbed my face.

"No. I- I hurt him." I cried.

"What? How?" She wiped my tears. "Show me."

I walked her down the stairs and over to his body.

"What happened?" She kneeled down in front of him.

"My life is over." I cried.

"What did you do?" She sat beside him.

"My- my life." I sobbed. "It's over. How do I explain this?"

"You don't." She stared up at me.

"What do you mean?" I cried. "I killed him!"

"First off, he's not dead. Secondly, you need to tell me and only me what happened." She reached into his pocket and grabbed his phone.

"What are you doing?" I watched her.

"I'm checking for any missed calls or texts from his parents." She explained. "Xena, the story."

"Right." I started to pace. "Well, remember the time when you and Dev were hooking up and magic was down? I was too pissed to tell you that he tried to assault me. Isis and the girls ended up coming over and they decided they wanted to make a potion for me, for him. To get him to unlove me. And well they did-"

"And you snuck it to him tonight?" She sighed.

"Yes! But I promise you, I *promise* you, I didn't think it would hurt him. I would never hurt another being no matter how vile they are. You believe me right? Just say you believe me. You believe me right?" I rambled.

"Of course I believe you." She reached for my hand.

"What do we do?" I cried. "God, are we trauma bonding?"

"I just need you to breathe." She checked his pulse. "Go call Isis while I think. You need to make sure that she didn't put anything else in that potion of yours."

"Okay." I grabbed my phone and walked out.

"X? You coming back?" She answered.

"Not quite. I have a question and I don't need anything but the answer." I tried to control my breathing.

"Okay." She drawled.

"What all did you put in that potion?" I glanced over at the clock.

"Uh, a few roots and basics. Why?" She asked. "You did it?!"

"I said no questions." I barked. "I'm- I'm in trouble Isis."

"What happened? Do you need me to-"

"No! You can't be apart of this." I cut her off.

"I already am." She reminded me.

"I'll call you back. Do *not* come here." I hung up.

"Nothing out of the ordinary." I rushed back over to Veronica.

"That doesn't make any sense." She sighed.

"I know." I frowned. "And it's getting later and later. What do we do?"

"I don't know but can you do me a favor?" She stood up. "Next time give me a heads up when I'm going to be your accomplice."

"Got it. Sorry." I walked over to her.

"Look, I'm a human. The most I know about magic is from Charmed, okay?" She began to panic.

"I'm so sorry." I cried. "I regret it. I regret it so much."

"I know you do." She consoled me. "Now I need you to help me, help you. We're going to drag his body to the guest house."

"I don't-"

"We don't have time to second guess this right now!" She barked. "Grab an arm and pull."

"Okay." I nodded.

I did as I was told and helped drag him out, through the grass, and into the guest house. I didn't say a word. I couldn't even process what we were doing. I felt completely out of touch with reality.

We laid him in bed and Veronica disappeared. I stood there watching his still body. I couldn't believe that I was so careless. Me. The poster child for preppy, the prude. I did this to this arrogant, self centered, yet helpless being.

Veronica returned and placed champagne and a bottle of pills next to him.

"Who's pills are those?" I spoke softly.

"Mine." She ripped off the label and stuffed it in her bra.

"All of this stress can't be good for the baby." I sighed.

"And me losing you wouldn't be good for any of us." She scattered the pills.

"Now help me get some into his mouth." She ordered.

"What? Why?" I stepped back. "Wouldn't that hurt him further?"

"Think about it Xena, if we're trying to stage this he needs to have some in his system." She sat down next to him.

"I guess that makes the most sense." I hesitantly stepped forward. "What do you need me to do?"

"Hold his mouth open while I shove them down." She instructed me.

I sat down on the other side of him and forced his mouth open while she stuck her hand down his throat. I could see how uncomfortable she was and the guilt began to wash over me again.

"Xena, focus." She snapped at me. "The pills are down. Pour some alcohol in."

"Okay." I grabbed the bottle and carefully poured it.

"Slow and steady or else he can choke." She guided me.

"But he's not conscious." I looked over at her.

"Slow and steady." She repeated.

When I was done, she grabbed the bottle from me and made me go wash my hands while she made sure everything was staged right. My hands shook uncontrollably as I washed them.

"Lets go." She walked into the bathroom.

We walked back into the house and into the living room. Veronica disposed of the table set up while I found a movie for us to watch. She wanted us to pretend that we had a normal night catching up and watching our favorite films which made complete sense. All we had to do was wait for my parents to get home.

Time went by so slow, I was sitting on the edge on the couch too anxious to relax. Veronica made me some tea to relax me but it wasn't working. Instead I stuffed my face full of extra butter popcorn.

"You're going to regret that in the morning." She smirked.

"Add it to the list." I sighed.

"It'll be okay." She grabbed my hand. "More popcorn?"

"Yes, please." I handed her the bowl.

As soon as she disappeared, I heard a car pull up in front.

"Uh, V." I whispered.

"Coming!" She shouted over the microwave beeping.

"Cover up!" I said just as the door opened.

"Xena." My mother smiled. "Look Hon, it's Xena."

"Hello." My father stormed past me.

"Hi." I waved.

"Hello Xena." Dax's parents greeted me warmly.

"Hi, did you guys have a good time?" I smiled.

"The best." His mother grinned. "Thanks for asking."

"Yes Xena, thank you." His father chimed in. "Well if you don't mind, we're going to turn in for the night."

"But I thought we were going to have that glass of wine so you could tell us about your trip abroad." My mother slipped off her shoes.

"Lead the way." His father smirked.

I crept upstairs and into my room hoping I wouldn't get called back down. I climbed into bed and buried myself under the covers. I couldn't help but cry. It was only a matter of time before it all hit the fan and the real acting began. I wasn't ready, I just wanted it to all go away. I cried for hours anticipating what I knew was coming.

"My baby!" I heard Dax's mother cry out.

I rushed downstairs and saw Dax being wheeled out on a stretcher by the medics. Everyone was surrounding him. I made eye contact with Veronica whose eyes were filled with remorse.

"Xena, go upstairs. I don't want you to see this." My mother looked up at me.

"What happened to him?" I frowned.

"He overdosed!" His mother blurted.

"Xena, now." My father ordered. "We'll talk later."

"How could this have happened? He was just so happy." I heard his Mother say as I closed my door.

Before I could break down, Veronica walked through my door.

"Hold it together." She whispered. "We're not in the clear until the hospital confirms it."

"I feel so bad." I whispered back.

"Don't fall apart. You didn't mean to do it. Continue to tell yourself that. You didn't make the potion. You just gave it to him. That is your only fault here." She reassured me.

"This isn't me. A boys life is on the line because of me." I cried.

"She needs to get down here right now!" My father bellowed. "Xena!"

"Just breathe." Veronica wiped my tears. "Don't say too much."

I nodded and walked out. I peered over the staircase and my father was sitting on the couch with his face in his hands. I took a deep breath and headed down the stairs.

"Yes?" I spoke over my rising anxiety.

"Xena." My mother hugged me.

"Don't hug her just yet." My father stood up.

"I'm just glad it wasn't her Brice." She scoffed.

"I'm more concerned about where she was." He crossed his arms.

"I was-"

"Don't you dare lie!" He yelled.

"Why is that every time something happens, you question me! I was watching movies with Veronica! You couldn't tell by the popcorn smell and the movie playing when you walked in?" I cried.

"Convenient." He snarled.

"Brice! That is enough." My mother stepped in front of me.

"I want to know every step you've made the moment you left the St. Nolend's. There is a being fighting for his life! This isn't a game! My reputation is on the line! This falls back on us, on me!" He argued.

"Of course! It's always about what you look like to beings that don't even matter! You don't care about them so why do you care what they think?" I sobbed. "I literally came inside, watched a few movies with Veronica, stuffed my face with extra buttered popcorn and talked about her time she was away and how much I missed her."

"I don't know." He sighed.

"You never believe me. Why don't you just send me with Veronica next time? You don't even want me here! I serve no purpose besides polishing your image! I'm tired Father. I'm 17 and tired! If you don't trust me, fine. I've given you zero reasons to question me and you still find someway to make me seem guilty. Well the feeling is mutual. I don't trust you either!" I stormed off.

"We're not finished!" He started after me.

"Brice." My mother stopped him. "Let her go."

XIII: INIQUITOUS

Seeing Dax in the hospital ripped my heart from my body. He was officially in a coma because of me. Thankfully our plan worked but investigators were still sniffing around and waiting for him to wake up. A part of me was hoping that he didn't as terrible as it made me feel.

I hadn't left my room other than to visit him. It had been two weeks and I was falling apart. I had to play the part with my parents but I truly couldn't stand myself. Guilt consumed me as soon as I was alone. I didn't eat, barely slept. I isolated myself entirely. The only being I spoke to was Veronica. My mental capacity was shrinking. I couldn't handle anything. Even a thread being loose on my blanket sent me spinning. I needed to step outside of myself but I didn't know how. I was stuck.

"Xena!" Isis and Zoe ran into my room.

"You look awful." Zoe frowned.

"Thank you." I turned away from them.

"Good going." Isis mumbled.

"X." She put her hand on my shoulder.

"Just go." I shrugged her off.

She backed away but I could still feel her eyes on me.

"Nope." She snatched my blankets off.

"What are you doing?" I curled in a ball.

"Not this." She opened my curtains and pulled my blinds.

"Can you not?" I winced from the brightness.

"Your wallowing days are over." She tried to pull me from the bed.

"No." I refused.

"Zoe? A little help here." She struggled.

"Right." Zoe grabbed my other arm.

They pulled me off the bed and we collapsed onto the floor.

"That was step one." Isis said as she stood up.

"Why are you guys here?" I pulled my knees to my chest.

"Why do you think?" Zoe smiled at me.

"You've literally iced us out for weeks. It's time to thaw out." Isis snatched me up.

"I can stand on my own." I muttered.

"Now for step two." She sat me down. "Look at me."

I looked all around the room before meeting her eyes. She looked so hopeful, so full of life. I knew what she was trying to do but it wasn't going to work.

"This was not your fault." She grabbed my hands. "You couldn't have known this was going to backfire. You had no parts of making that stupid potion. All you wanted was him out of your way. He humiliated you time and time again. He embarrassed you on live television for all dimensions to see. He deserved it."

"He didn't deserve to die!" I cried.

"And you didn't try to kill him!" She shook me.

"Doesn't matter!" I pushed her off and walked over to my window.

"It does." Zoe added. "Your intentions weren't for that to happen. If anything this is our fault."

"100% and if the time comes, we are prepared to take the-"

"No!" I turned around. "You can't, I won't let you!"

"If you don't pull yourself out of this, you won't have a choice. We will turn ourselves into the council. Nothing you can do about it." She shrugged.

"And who do you think they'll believe? Us or you? The perfect little daughter of Brice and Azura or the semi delinquents that sneak out after curfew?" Zoe wiped my tears.

"Why are you doing this?" I continued to sob.

"Because we love you." Isis made my bed. "We're in this together."

"Step three." Zoe smiled. "You need to eat."

"I can't." I shook my head.

"You can and you will." Isis grabbed my hand. "If I have to threaten our livelihood every step of the way, I will. You are going to eat. You are going to forgive yourself. You are going to let us help you or else you will watch us all go down. If you comply, we'll be safe. What happens here on out is on you. It takes nothing for me to turn myself in."

"And you know she's serious." Zoe grabbed my other hand.

"I know." I nodded.

"So, Veronica has prepared your favorites. Let's go." They pulled me out the room.

"Hey love." Veronica greeted me.

The girls continued to the table and I walked around over to her.

"Hi." I hugged her and secretly rubbed her stomach. "How are you?"

"Doing okay." She nodded. "French toast?"

"Yes, please." I smirked.

"Go. I'm right behind you." She grabbed the platter and orange juice.

I joined the girls at the table. They were talking about Sarai. I was so wrapped up in my problems that I had completely abandoned Sarai's.

"What about Sarai?" I asked as I poured juice in my cup.

"They let her go." Isis smiled.

"When was she ever-"

"Yeah, you missed a lot." Zoe sighed. "They detained her but they had to let her go due to lack of evidence."

"But she's still confined to her room. She can't leave the house." Isis poured champagne into the orange juice.

"One glass." Veronica placed the French toast between us.

"Of course." I smiled at her. "I just feel so bad for Sarai."

"But things are looking up for her and that's all we can ask for." Veronica smiled back. "Everything gets better."

"You hear that X?" Isis nudged me. *"Everything."*

"Right." I said sarcastically.

"Now, what are we doing today?" Zoe smirked.

"Nothing." I poured syrup on her plate.

"Something." Isis chewed.

"Veronica, what's on the schedule today?" I looked over at her.

"For you, nothing. For your parents, two meetings and-"

"I stopped listening after me." I cut into my food.

"I'm proud of you for eating." She ignored my comment.

"Have you talked to Oscar?" Zoe winked.

"Who's Oscar?" Isis sipped her drink.

"Oscar." She kicked her under the table.

"You can say his name." I chuckled dryly. "Veronica knows. But no. I haven't. Not since Isis stole my phone time. What did he say to you?"

"Nothing much after that besides he misses you a lot and for you to call him back." She revealed. "I really just wanted to talk to Rowan."

"You're just now telling me?" I rolled my eyes. "He's going to think I didn't want to talk to him!"

"Sorry?" She shrugged. "It slipped my mind."

"I'll be upstairs." I walked away.

I searched through my duffle bag until I found the phone. I had 3 missed calls from Owen and a facemail from an unsaved number. I locked my door and called Owen.

"Hi." He said warmly.

"I'm so sorry I've been distant. A lot has happened." I sat down.

"Talk to me. I'm listening." He encouraged me.

We talked for hours and I didn't leave out any details. I didn't feel judged, I didn't feel rushed. I felt heard. I forgot how good Owen made me feel. How good love felt. He told me that he could help Dax but it would take a few days. I didn't question him. I trusted every word he uttered. He said that he started working at the office and that they missed me there. I knew that they didn't but I sent my love anyway and promised I would be there tomorrow. Our call was interrupted by his father walking in. It ended so abruptly I didn't get a chance to say goodbye.

I tucked the phone back in my bag and laid down on the bed.

It was hard to place what I was feeling. I just knew that I was happy I got to talk to Owen. It was the first positive emotion I'd felt in a long time. I knew that I was grateful for Isis and Zoe, especially Veronica. Everything else was a blur.

"Welcome back!" Balic and Margo greeted me as I stepped out of the elevator.

"Yes, welcome." Jen stormed off.

"We totally missed Team Ion Galactica in full effect." Margo smiled.

"We didn't even get to see our full potential." I frowned.

"Well, we saw a little glimpse of what you could do, you're a valuable component to our team." Balic complimented me. "Now let's head in before Jen tears our heads off."

"After you." Margo held the door for me.

As soon as I walked in, my eyes locked on Owen. He was sitting in my seat but I didn't mind. Before I could sit down next to him, Lindsay brushed past me and plopped down in the seat.

"Sorry Xena, were you planning on sitting here?" She looked over at me.

"I'm actually staring at the being in my chair." I smiled at Owen.

"Xi- I mean, Xena, Hi." He stood up. "Seats yours. I was just keeping it warm for you."

"Thank you." I walked over and sat down.

His cologne made my knees weak as he hovered over me to push my chair in.

"You're very welcome." He took his seat across from me.

"I'm sorry Lindsay, did you plan on staying here?" I mocked her.

"No." She stormed off.

"Listen up beings, Mr. Briarwood has new assignments for everyone. Turn your attention to him." Jen opened the door and in walked my Father.

"Hello all." He stood at the end of the table. "I'll make this short and sweet. New assignments, new partners."

"Ion Galactica." Margo whined.

"We had a good run." Balic put his hand on her shoulder.

"Basically we need a writer and a runner. The runner is the being that answers the calls, the writer jots everything down and turns it into an article. A wonderfully written masterpiece that will be printed in our newspaper." My father explained. "Pretty simple work. Any questions?"

"Do we get to pick our partners?" Balic grinned.

"No. I've already assigned them. Go look at the list on the wall." He instructed.

Everyone rushed over to see who their partners were. I stayed in my seat and waited for my partner to approach me.

"Xena, the list?" My father cleared his throat.

"Can't you just tell me?" I sighed.

"Yeah, it's-"

"Me." Owen said behind me.

"I feel you two would make a viable team. I know what you both are capable of and I expect the best." My father closed his briefcase and walked out.

"This was rigged!" Lindsay pouted.

"Would you like to tell that to the boss?" Jen stepped in front of her.

"No thank you." She frowned.

"Great. Partner up, find a room." She dismissed us.

"So, partners huh?" Owen whispered.

"Yeah." I blushed. "Come on, we can go to my favorite room."

I led the way and I could feel him watching me. I didn't mind. I actually liked it. I walked him into the first room I worked in with Balic and Margo. I knew Owen would appreciate the beauty of this room.

"Welcome to my favorite room!" I stepped in.

"It's beautiful." He stared at the artwork beneath his feet.

"I know. That's why it's my favorite." I smirked as I closed the door.

"You're my favorite." He pushed me up against the door.

"Say it again." I kissed him.

"You." He pulled me close. "Are my favorite."

We kissed passionately until we were interrupted by our first caller. I rushed over to the phone and picked it up. Owen pulled out his notebook and waited to take notes.

"Hello, thank you for calling BSDR. How may I help you?" I smiled.

"My name is Roux and I'm calling to report a potential crime." The caller spoke.

"Please tell me what happened." I pulled out a pen to take notes of my own.

"Well, my cousin, Uma, she's been working for the council for about four years now and she loved her job, really. She didn't want anything but to make the council happy." He explained.

"Go on." I glanced over at Owen who was scribbling on his notepad.

"She found something. Something big. I told her to hold off but she insisted on meeting with them. I wanted to go with her but they are so secretive they didn't even let me near the car they sent for her. I haven't seen her since." He sniffled.

"I'm so sorry to hear that." I said sincerely. "When did this happen?"

"Four days ago." He cried. "I'm so worried. This isn't like her. What if they did something to her?"

"I understand. I'm going to take down all your information and forward it to my boss. She will then call you back and explain the next steps-"

"Which are? I mean, how long do I have to wait?" He sputtered.

"Not long. And I just want to tell you, you have every right to be upset. Let that drive you not destroy you, okay? You will be hearing from us soon. I promise." I said before he hung up.

"You're a natural." Owen smirked.

"So I've been told." I winked.

"I should get started on my article, huh?" He walked over to the computer.

"Yeah. More calls should be rolling in soon." I sighed. "It never stops."

We worked for hours straight with minimal conversation in between. It was a rough day. The calls were non stop. Owen seemed to handle the load with ease. He had his entire assignment completed before lunch. There were so many cases, he had to choose which to publish. I could see the anguish in his face. This was as personal for him as it was for me. And even though he didn't talk about it, I knew it was triggering. I just hope it was helping more than it was hurting.

After he printed his paper, we sat down and talked about Sarai and Dax.

"If it gets too bad, I can hide her in my dimension." He offered.

"I don't want you to get dragged into this." I shook my head.

"I'd do anything for you, Xi." He grabbed my hand.

"I know." I leaned on his shoulder.

"So let me help you." He whispered.

"So you're just going to solve all my problems?" I looked at him.

"If I can." He nodded. "If you let me."

"Incoming." He sat up and released my hand.

"Owen!" Lindsay interrupted. "Hi!"

"Hey." He smiled.

"Hi, I just wanted to come and see how your day went." She twirled her hair.

"It was eventful." He chuckled. "Xena's amazing. She did all the heavy lifting. I just typed."

"Right." She glanced over at me. "Anyway, a few of us were going to go get a bite to eat, would you want to come? Boss approved."

I pulled out my phone and pretended not to care.

"Uh, no thanks." He sighed. "Today's been long and I need to talk to Xena about some things."

"Things?" She tried to hide her irritation. "She can come if she wants."

"She doesn't." I said still looking at my phone.

"Come on, Owen." She rubbed his arm.

"Thanks again for the invite but no." He stood up and walked over to his desk.

"Well, can I at least turn in your assignment for you? I have to talk to Jen anyway." She walked over to him.

"Sure. That would be great." He sighed with a smile. "Thank you."

"Anytime." She grabbed his folder and walked out.

"See you tomorrow." I said sarcastically.

"Be nice." He smiled.

"I am nice. I didn't tell her that she was trying way too hard. Therefore, I'm nice." I simpered.

"Fair enough." He chuckled. "You know, me turning her down to talk to you will raise some brows."

"I don't care if you don't." I watched him walk over. "But I do have to go."

"Why?" He blocked my exit.

"Because if I don't beat my dad home there will be a million questions and a round for round shouting match. I'm too exhausted to argue with him." I packed up my things.

"Tomorrow?" He handed me my laptop.

"Tomorrow." I nodded.

"Can I walk you out?" He grinned.

"I don't think that's a good idea." I looked up at him.

"Neither is us working together." He put his cool hands on my waist. "Still have my shirt?"

"Of course I do." I whispered.

"Xena! Your father wants you!" Someone shouted.

"Gotta go." I slung my bag over my shoulder and walked out.

I headed into my fathers office and waited for him to get off of the phone but he didn't even acknowledge me. After 20 minutes of me twiddling my thumbs, I decided to interrupt him.

"I'll see you at home." I stood up.

"Sit down." He demanded.

"I'll be in the car with Lars." I stormed out.

"Good evening." Lars opened my door.

"Hi." I hugged him as I got in.

"How was your day?" He climbed in next to me.

"It was rough but rewarding." I sighed.

"Where's your father?" He handed me a water bottle.

"Thank you." I forced a smile. "He's inside. Talking to whomever."

"I'm going to get back in the front before he tears me a new one." He slid out the backseat.

"Yeah, I'm just going to close my eyes for a second." I kicked my feet up.

I loved being with Lars. It was similar to being with Veronica. I felt supported, comforted. I didn't feel the incessant need to be perfect. Father would've slapped my feet down in a second. Instead, Lars placed his back pillow under my legs for comfort.

"Father's coming." Lars tapped me awake.

"Thank you." I sat up quickly.

"Xena." My father opened the door. "Get out."

"What?" I scoffed.

"Get. Out." He ordered.

I stepped out into the cold weather and waited for him to speak.

"Before you rudely dismissed yourself, I was going to tell you that you're going somewhere." He started. "You're going on a college trip this weekend."

"For what college? Why?" I asked confused.

"I have a business trip to take this weekend and frankly I don't trust you home alone anymore. I don't need any trouble while I'm gone, I'm in enough as is." He explained.

Something told me that he wasn't telling me the full truth. It was too random, too sudden. Father was always calculated. He was up to something.

"Father, I know you think I'm this liar and deceiver that I've never been, but that can't be the only reason why you are sending me away." I finally looked him in the eyes. "Can you just tell me what's going on?"

"Thats the first time you actually looked at me in weeks." He sighed. "You're right. There's another reason, a bigger reason. A reason I'm not sure you can handle."

"I can handle it." I avowed. "Just trust me."

"It's Sarai." He confessed.

"What about her?" I stepped towards him.

"I tried my hardest to prove that she wasn't involved but the council believes what they want to." He looked off.

"What does that mean?" Tears streamed down my face.

"They're going to convict her, Honey." He sniffled. "Theres nothing I can do."

"But she's innocent!" I cried.

"I know." He hugged me. "I just need you far away from here. I don't need you caught up in this. She's going to be extradited this weekend. You and I will be away from here. The council can't confirm your alibi from when he was killed and I don't need them poking around in our lives next. Please, I know this is hard but don't give them a reason to."

I listened to everything he was saying. He was actually being kind. Something he's never been. He was being a father. I leaned into it. I needed the comfort, I was tired of fighting with him. As sweet as he was being, my plan to help Sarai was still intact.

"I don't want to fight with you Xena, I just want to protect you at all costs." He sighed.

"Is there anything we can do to help her?" I sobbed.

"No. Not now. We have to let them do what they've planned. When she's sentenced, then we can try and help her." He kissed the top of my head. "Let's go home."

"Okay." I sniffled as he helped me into the car.

XIV: COMMISERATION

I spent all night tossing and turning. I couldn't believe that Sarai was going to be ripped from us. I wanted to tip her off but everyone was under a microscope. I couldn't risk it if I planned to let Owen help me. I didn't want any reason for the council to question me. I was already trying to pull off the impossible. I secretly told Owen everything last night when I called him. Thankfully, he was still onboard.

Last night was the first night in years that I felt at home in my home. My parents and I actually had a civilized conversation over dinner. They comforted me. We even shared a few laughs. Mother helped me pack all the things I wanted and lied to Father about them appropriate, which was completely unlike her. Who knew that when tragedy struck, they would come through for me.

I truly didn't want to show my face at work. I had no drive to do my job. I didn't want to spend my time answering phones and helping beings when I couldn't even help keep my best friend out of trouble. I knew she wouldn't tell the truth and give up the WGW's location. She was more solid than that. She would rather go down, than to take us all down with her. I admired her for that. I had to save her.

"Hi." Owen greeted me as I walked into the conference room.

Everyone already in their seats listening to Jen. I didn't care that I distracted everyone from her presentation. I walked in with my shades on and took my seat.

"Thank you for joining us, Xena." She huffed.

"You're very welcome." I said in the same tone.

"Like I was saying, Mr. Briarwood had a chance to take a look at your stats and he was very pleased with most of you." She continued. "And honestly, so am I. Give yourself a round of applause."

Everyone started clapping while I just sat there watching.

Owen stared at me with a concerning look that I couldn't engage with. I pretended I didn't see him and kept looking forward.

"Right away, Sir." Jen spoke into her headset.

"Mr. Briarwood is on his way up. He will announce the group with the highest stats and introduce us to a new team member." She sat down at the head of the table.

We all turned our attention to my Father stepping out the elevator.

"Good morning team." He walked into the conference room.

"Good morning Mr. Briarwood." We all chimed.

"Lets jump in because I have a meeting in 10." He sipped his coffee. "First, the team with the highest stats. I was truly impressed with the numbers, the efficiency and the structure."

"Who was it, Sir?" Tomas asked eagerly.

"Xena and Owen." He announced.

"So biased." Some-being scoffed.

"I'm sorry, do you have a problem with my announcement? Do you think our system is rigged?" He sat down on the edge of the table.

"I just-"

"Pack your things and go." He simpered.

"But-" He stood up.

"But nothing. Turn your badge in at the front desk and get the hell out." He opened my briefcase.

"I'm sorry Mr. Briarwood." He packed his things.

"And I'm sorry I didn't learn your name so that I could fire you properly." He shooed him.

"Bye everyone." He ran out.

Everyone remained quiet, too afraid of expulsion.

"Now, back to what I was saying." My father smiled. "Xena and Owen, you two did amazing. Owen, your Father was right about you being an overachiever, and Xena, you truly never fail me. We got nothing but stellar reviews about your hospitality and empathy towards the victims. Give them a round of applause."

"Alright Owen!" Ryland clapped louder than everyone else.

"Ion Galactica honors your win." Balic smiled at me.

"Don't be weird." Margo nudged him. "Great job, Xena."

"Thank you." I smiled.

"Everyone else, you were great. Let's see what you can do today. If the numbers come back just as high, you'll stay partnered, if not, we need to regroup. If you have any questions or need any tips, go to Xena and Owen. They know what they're doing." My father grinned.

"In other news, I want you to meet someone very near and dear to my heart, my beautiful and talented Goddaughter, Isis St. Nolend!"

My face lit up as I saw her walk in. She looked just as beautiful as ever. I'd never seen her in a blazer but she wore it with grace. I watched her proudly.

"Hello everyone." She spoke softly as she stood behind him.

"I should've saved my applause for her." Ryland smirked.

"She's beautiful." I heard another girl say.

"Can I get paid in her?" Tomas flirted.

"That's enough." Jen barked. "Have some class."

"You're just mad that we're not all over you." Ryland grinned.

"Introduce yourself, Isis." My father guided her in front of him.

"Hello, I'm Isis St. Nolend. I'm here to assist you all. Together we will find a way to end BSD. I am very knowledgable on the topic. My father and I have been looking into a few cases of our own. Basically I'm just here to help." She smiled.

"Treat her as you would treat me. She is just as valuable." My father kissed her forehead. "She will be teaming up with Xena and Owen but will be available to all groups. She will be watching and reporting back to me. Make me proud. That's all for now."

Everyone dispersed into their groups. Owen and I walked Isis to our office and locked the door.

"Nice room." She sat down at the round table.

"Yeah." I nodded as I sat down next to her.

"Does she know?" Owen kissed me.

"Do I know what?" She looked at me.

"No. She doesn't." I sighed.

"Hello." She waved. "*She* is sitting right here. What don't I know?"

"About Sarai." I took off my shades.

"What happened now, X?" She frowned. "Look at your eyes, they're so puffy."

"I know." I fought my tears. "She's-"

"Is she dead?" She stood up. "She's what, Xena?"

I couldn't answer. I broke down in tears as I struggled to.

"She's going to be extradited tomorrow." Owen spoke for me.

"No fucking way." Isis gasped.

"Yes but we have a plan." He put his arm around me.

"We do?" She smiled. "Oh, I am so in."

"Don't be so eager." I sniffled. "It's a risk for all of us."

"And she's worth that risk." She crossed her arms.

"I know." I nodded.

"Xi." Owen wiped my tears.

His cool touch was so comforting. He looked so concerned for me. I loved the way he cared for me. The way he handled me.

"Thank you." I leaned on his shoulder.

"That was cute." Isis smirked. "So, what's the plan?"

"I just need a minute." I walked into the bathroom.

I needed to get my emotions together. I had to think smart. And to think smart I had to think clearly. There was no room for error in this plan. It had to be perfect from start to finish.

I gathered myself and walked out of the bathroom.

"You okay, X?" Isis rushed over to me.

"No." I embraced her.

Isis literally never cried. The only time I saw her cry was when she lost her grandparents, since then, not a tear. She was the nurturer and the solider of our group. She was resilient. Her breaking down in my arms broke my heart.

"Owen." She pulled away from me. "I'm not a crier, I promise."

"It's fine, I get it. She's your best friend." He assured her.

"She is." She nodded. "So, what's this plan?"

"Plan is, we go over to Sarai's house and you distract her mom while Sarai and I open up a portal in her room. That portal will take her to Owen's. He will hide her out there until we can prove she's innocent." I explained.

"Easy." She grabbed my hand and walked back over to the table.

"It won't be." I sighed. "But it's the only plan we've got that'll work."

"Did you hear about my dad sending me away for the weekend?" She changed the subject.

"Yeah, you're going with me." I forced a smile.

"So, our parents planned this together." She rolled her eyes.

"Yup." I nodded.

"Well, at least you'll have solid alibi's." Owen chimed in.

"That's true." She pulled out her phone.

"My dad leaves tonight. We'll do it after he leaves." I looked at Owen.

He had an unreadable expression on his face. I wanted to ask what was wrong but I knew he was a private being and he wasn't exactly comfortable expressing how he felt.

"Who are you texting?" I grabbed her free hand.

"My mom. I'm going to tell her I'm going to be here late." She continued to type. "You should do the same."

"You should." Owen nodded.

I pulled out my phone and texted Mother and Veronica against my better judgment. The phone began to ring, stopping me from pressing send. I took that as a sign and locked my phone.

I rushed over to my desk and answered the call.

"Well Isis, welcome to hell." Owen smiled.

"I'm familiar." She smirked back.

We worked all day as usual but I was visibly distracted. Isis picked up my slack with ease. I just couldn't stop thinking about the plan. If we could pull it off, if Owen would get caught, if Sarai would even go with it. All of those things rang in my head until we clocked out.

We waited for everyone to leave before we discussed the minor, yet viable details.

"Owen, you should leave first. It'll seem odd if the three of us stay behind." Isis suggested.

"Okay." He started to pack his things.

"Isis, can I talk to Owen in private for a second?" I walked over to him.

"Yes." She walked out with her phone in hand.

"Can I ask you something?" I sat on the edge of his desk.

"Yes." He continued to pack.

"Are you sure you're okay with this?" I stared at him.

"My only concern is you." He answered coldly.

"Then why-"

"Nothing can happen to you. I won't survive it, Xi." He sighed.

"Nothing will." I grabbed his face.

He leaned into my hand and I pulled his face close to mine.

"Nothing will." I said again.

He kissed me so passionately, I almost lost my balance. He kissed me as if it was the last time he would see me. I could see the fear in his face, I wanted to erase it.

I slid on top of the desk and pulled him between my legs, our lips never unlocking. He climbed on top of me and gently pressed his body against mine.

"I can't lose you." He whispered.

"You never will." I whispered back as he kissed my neck.

"Xena!" Isis knocked on the door. "Sorry to interrupt."

"Coming!" I shouted back.

I tried to stand up but he pushed me back down.

"Just five more minutes." He put his hand around my neck and unbuttoned my shirt.

"Welcome back." Isis hid her smile as we walked in.

"Ready to do this?" I forced the rosiness from my cheeks.

"Nope." She smiled.

"I'll head out. Xi, keep your phone nearby." He kissed me.

"I will." I nodded.

"See you soon, Isis." He smiled before walking out.

"Send Rowan my love!" She yelled after him.

"You're ridiculous." I chuckled.

"Your father is still here." Isis whispered.

"And you said that out loud?" I scolded her.

"It was innocent." She shrugged. "I've been to their house with my father."

"You have?" I scoffed.

"I have." She winked.

"Let's go see my Father." I pulled her by the hand.

"Girls." He met us at the door. "Come in."

"We can't stay Father, I'm training Isis. Pretending to be the caller and seeing how she interacts." I lied.

"Oh yeah?" He looked over at Isis. "And how's she doing?"

"Surprisingly well." I smiled.

"Okay well, I'm leaving from the office. Owen's dad and I are going to a business retreat and I'll be there to pick you up when your campus visit is over. Veronica and your mother will see you off. Understood?" He kissed both of our heads. "See you soon."

"See you." I watched him until he was gone.

"Are we taking Lars?" She closed his office door.

"I don't know, I don't want to implicate him." I rubbed my temples.

"But anyone else would run to the council as soon as they see what's going on." She reminded me.

"True." I sighed. "We have to."

"He's waiting outside for us, isn't he?" She peered out the window.

"Of course he is." I reached for her hand.

"Anything for Sarai." She placed her hand in mine.

We walked outside and over to the truck. Lars was asleep. I slid into the front seat and Isis climbed in the back.

"Hey." He sat up.

"Okay, I need your help with this very important thing but I can't tell you what that thing is because I don't want you to get in any trouble-"

"Enough said." He started the car. "Where am I going?"

"Sarai's house. Stealth mode." I put on my seatbelt.

"You rock Lars!" Isis cheered.

When we pulled up to Sarai's, Lars hid the car as best as he could and turned the lights off.

"You ready?" I looked back at Isis.

"I really wish you would stop asking me that." She got out.

"We'll be back." I promised Lars before running after Isis.

Isis knocked on the door and took a deep breath. My heart raced as we waited for someone to answer. One of Sarai's brothers answered the door shirtless.

"Hey boys, our deliveries here!" He shouted to his brothers.

Another one ran up and pulled the door open.

"Didn't order them but I'm not complaining." He nudged his brother.

"Get out of our way." Isis pushed past them.

"Wheres your mom?" I looked around.

"Xena!" Her little sister ran up and hugged my legs. "Mama's in the kitchen."

"Thank you." I rubbed her back and headed for the kitchen with Isis.

Sarai's mom was standing at the island drinking wine out the bottle. Her hair was a mess and the kitchen was worse. I felt so bad just looking at her. We awkwardly stood in the archway.

"Hello." Mrs. Orozco smiled wryly. "What a surprise."

"Hi." I hugged her.

"Oh Xena, Sarai will be so happy to see you two." She stroked my hair.

"We just wanted to come by and say hello." I signaled Isis to take over.

"Hi Mrs. O! Where's my hug?" Isis hugged her from behind.

"Yes. There's one for you too!" She turned around and drunkenly embraced her.

"Can I get you another drink?" Isis pulled her over to the table.

I crept out of the room and up the stairs. I only had a finite amount of time to do this. I walked into her room and she was sitting on her floor sobbing.

"Xena?" She looked up at me.

I pulled her a duffle bag from the back of her door and started packing every piece of clothing I saw.

"What the hell are you doing?" She stood up.

"Packing. Let's go. You're getting out of here." I walked into her bathroom to grab her toiletries.

"What? No!" She argued.

"Do you want to be in purgatory for the rest of your life? No? Then help me pack your shit. I'm trying to save you." I whispered angrily.

"Where are we going?" She asked as she helped me.

"You're going. *You*." I corrected her.

"Where?" She asked again.

"I can't tell you that." I zipped her bag and grabbed her hands. "But you need to know that I love you and where you're going, they'll keep you safe."

"Okay." She hugged me.

"Now go set up a portal in your bathroom, I'll meet you in there." I stuffed a family photo in the side of her bag.

"I can't. They took my powers." She whimpered.

"We're going to have to do this the hard way then." I sighed. "Do you still remember the invisibility spell?"

"Yes." She nodded.

"Do it. I need to make a phone call." I rushed into her bathroom and called Owen.

"Xi?" He answered.

"We have a problem." I began to pace back and forth. "They took her powers, she can't set up the portal and I can't do it from her house, they'll track me."

"Do you-"

"Hold on. My moms calling." I pulled my phone from my back pocket.

"Yes?" I tried to answer as calmly as possible.

"I need you home. Now." She hung up.

My heart began to race as the panic set in.

"Owen?" I wiped my tears.

"I heard." He sighed. "Can you have Isis meet me at The Revolution?"

"Yes but-"

"But nothing." He cut me off. "Have her meet me. You go home."

"Okay." I tried to breathe through my anxiety. "Okay."

"Talk soon." The line went dead.

I walked back into the room and Sarai was nowhere in sight.

"Over here." She whispered.

"Perfect. It worked." I walked towards her voice.

"Basic spells only. No teleporting, no portals." She sighed.

"Good enough. Let's head downstairs. Stay close to me." I threw her bag out the window.

"Okay." She linked arms with me.

We walked out of her room slowly. I didn't want to move too fast or draw attention to us. Her brothers were roaming around, if one of them got close enough, our plan would be exposed.

"Go get your bag and wait by the car." I whispered before I pushed her out the front door.

"Is that our pizza?" Her little brother ran down the stairs.

"Afraid not." I closed the door. "Just me. Getting some air."

"They're never coming." He stormed back up the stairs.

"Isis!" I called out.

"Be quiet." She darted around the corner. "I just got her to sleep."

"Sorry." I pulled her close. "She's outside, let's go."

"You're amazing." She smirked.

We crept out the front door and ran over to Lars.

"Ready to go?" He rolled down the window.

"Uh, X?" Isis looked around. "I don't spy a Sarai."

"Behind you." Sarai whispered.

"Whoa." She stepped back.

"Now you know how I felt my first night at the warehouse." I opened the back door. "Get in."

"You are the smartest friend. I love you." Isis grinned as she got in.

"Sarai?" I waited for her to get in.

"I'm in!" She answered.

"Great." I slid in the passenger seat. "Let's go Lars. Home."

"Home?" They all said in sync.

"Is there an echo in here?" Lars looked in the rearview mirror.

"Yeah. Mother's orders. If I don't show, it's my ass." I sighed.

"We understand." Isis simpered.

"So, you guys are going to meet-" I looked over at Lars. "You know who at work and do it from there."

"Okay." Isis nodded.

We all sat in silence. I was sure that Isis and Sarai were just as afraid as I was but it was too late to turn back now. This was our only shot.

"We're home." Lars cleared his throat.

"Thank you, Lars. Work then Isis' house." I hugged him.

"Can you step out with me?" I looked back at Sarai.

"Sure." She whispered.

She opened her door and stepped out.

"I love you." I cried.

"I love you more." She grabbed my hands.

"Owen will be there waiting for you. Don't be scared, okay?" I hugged her.

"Okay." She sniffled.

"Xena, you have cameras and you look a little weird hugging the air." Isis scolded me.

"Right." I sighed. "Isis, call me when it's done."

"I will." She opened the door for Sarai.

"Bye." I blew her a kiss and ran inside.

I slipped off my shoes at the door and dropped my purse on the rack. I could hear Veronica and Mother talking in the kitchen.

"I'm home." I sighed.

"Xena." Veronica smiled. "You hungry?"

"Hello." Mother said warmly.

"Hello and no, not really." I sat down at the bar.

"Your father told me about your amazing performance as work." My mother clapped.

"We're so proud of you." Veronica hugged me.

"Thank you, V." I smiled.

"Veronica must've been eating off your celebration cake, she's looking a little bloated." My mother joked.

"I-"

"You got me a cake?" I saved Veronica. "What kind?"

"Cheesecake with chocolate truffles. Your favorite!" She exclaimed.

"So Xena, ready to start packing for the morning?" Veronica pulled the cake from the fridge.

"I already did. Last night." I spun around in the chair.

"Somebeing's eager." Mother chuckled.

"Yeah, it's finally a school I'm interested in." I lied.

"Well, Veronica and I will walk you through the portal but after that you're on your own." She cut me the smallest piece of cake.

"I know." I nodded.

"Eat your cake and head to bed." She slid the plate in front of me.

"Right." I took a bite.

"Smaller bites Honey, you'll get full faster." Mother winked.

"It's cake Mother, it's meant to be enjoyed." I rolled my eyes.

"Veronica would know." She said before walking out.

"Do you think she knows?" Veronica whispered.

"No. She's just a vibe killer." I sighed. "You look amazing."

"And that's why you're my favorite little witch." She smirked.

"If it wasn't clear before, I'm the Godmother." I chewed.

"Done. Can I go throw up now?" She ran out.

"Was it the cake?" I shouted after her.

My phone vibrated on the counter and I quickly answered it.

"It's done." Isis hung up.

I could finally exhale. I placed my dish in the sink and went to bed.

XVI: DENOUEMENT

"Rise and shine Babygirl! It's time to go meet those hot boys from the 1st dimension!" Isis jumped in my bed.

"Uh no, I have Owen." I turned away from her.

"Oh yeah, *Owen*." She tickled me.

"How can you be so chipper while our friend is on the run?" I pushed her off.

"Because I trust where she's at and we have to act like we didn't just commit the biggest crimes of our lives." She hit me with a pillow.

"You're right." I sighed. "Let's go get you some hot boys."

"That's the spirit." She shook me excitedly. "Get dressed. Breakfast and the portals waiting."

"Okay." I climbed out of bed.

I grabbed my robe and walked into the bathroom. I took the longest, hottest shower I could stand and just cried. I couldn't stop and I didn't want to. I just wanted to feel my feelings before I had to face a new day in a new place. I was tired of putting on this brave face as if nothing was wrong. Everything was. I sat down on the shower floor and gave into my emotions.

"Out the shower. Now." Isis snatched the curtain open. "Xena."

"I'm fine." I looked up at her.

"No you're not." She turned the water off.

"I am." I cried. "Just go."

"You should know me better than that." She climbed in the tub with me. "It's just a little water."

"What are you doing?" I sighed.

"Holding you." She sat behind me and wrapped her arms around my wet body. "I love you."

"I love you." I leaned into her.

"It's going to be okay." She held me tighter. "We're going to get away from all this madness and press pause. We're going to see what the human world has to offer us. We can't blow this. This could be our chance to get away. For good."

"You're right." I nodded. "I'm trying to pull it together, I promise."

"I know." She sniffled.

"I don't know how you're not falling apart." I looked up at her.

"Trust me, I'm not as put together as I seem." She whispered.

We just sat there for a while. We didn't talk. We didn't feel the need to fill the silence. We just existed and that's exactly what I needed. To just be. Eventually Isis forced me out of the tub and downstairs to eat. I wasn't in the mood to deal with Mother but I did restore enough strength to power through the day.

After breakfast Isis and I took our bags to the portal room and waited impatiently for Veronica and Mother to join us. Owen made sure to text me around the clock to let me know Sarai was okay. I couldn't wait until I could talk to him without looking over my shoulder.

"Are you feeling any better?" Isis rubbed my arm.

"Yeah, thank you for earlier. I needed it more than I know." I smirked.

"I needed it too." She picked up her bag. "How's Sam?"

"He's good." I played along.

"Who's ready to be the trustworthy, lovely ladies that we raised?" My mother walked in with Veronica behind her.

"We are." Isis sung.

"Let's go then." She closed the door.

I looked down and watched the blue lights seal the door.

"We're here!" Isis shrieked.

"Go on girls, open the door." My mother danced.

"Are you sure this isn't *your* college visit?" I rolled my eyes.

"So, I'll ignore that snarky little comment in the spirit of your first human college experience." She hugged me. "I love you. Go make me proud."

"Everyday." I said sarcastically as I opened the door.

"You'll do great." Veronica smiled.

We stepped into a hallway full of unfamiliar faces. It was definitely a college setting. Bustling halls, pretty girls with stressed out faces. It was everything I've seen in the movies. We didn't have actors and movies in our dimension. Every movie I've seen Veronica showed me. It always made me wonder how my life would be as an actress, as a human.

"Hello. Earth to Xena." Isis stepped in front of me. "While you were zoned out I got our room key. Let's go. We're on the next floor and I have a surprise for you."

"But you know I hate surprises." I groaned.

"Hello Frosh." A muscular guy approached us.

"Hey." Isis smiled.

"Gotta name?" He shook her hand and kissed it.

"Wouldn't you like to know." She pulled me into the elevator.

"You're such a tease." I rolled my eyes. "Also, can you please stop pulling me everywhere? I'm not four."

"Please. If I don't pull you, you won't move." She applied her lipgloss in the mirror.

"I know you're just being extra chipper to cheer me up." I admitted.

"So?" She shrugged.

"So, you can stop." I turned her to face me.

"No thank you." She pulled me out of the elevator.

"Isis." I groaned.

"302." She cheered. "That's us!"

"You're way too excited for me. I'm starting to think it's not an act." I rolled my eyes.

"Just open the door already." She pushed me.

I pushed the door open and she brushed past me and ran in.

"This is definitely a scene out of one of those movies where everyone dies in the end." I walked in and put my bag down.

The room was actually cute. Basic. But really cute. It had two full sized beds, two desks, two walk in closets and the most amazing view of the campus. I could get used to the set up.

"You like it? You love it?" She danced in front of me.

"Yeah, I like it." I sat down on my bed.

"And I got something else you'll like." She danced her way over to the closet.

"What? You ordered us matching shoe racks?" I rolled my eyes.

"Not shoe racks but you could definitely get a work out." She grinned.

She opened the door and Owen stepped out with Rowan. I sat there stunned and definitely surprised.

"Xi." He approached me.

"Rowan, hi." Isis pulled him in for a kiss.

"Come here." Rowan pulled her back into the closet and closed the door.

"What- What are you doing here?" I hugged Owen.

"I'm here to see you." He sat down next to me.

"Are you sure this is safe?" I asked as he kissed me.

"Yes. My father can't track us while he's traveling dimensions." He smiled. "And don't worry, Sarai is perfectly safe."

"Thank you." I hugged him again. "I'm so happy to see you."

"That was the reaction I was looking for the first time." He chuckled.

"Sorry. I'm just everywhere lately." I sighed.

"And that's okay. Lay with me for a minute." He kicked off his shoes and slid into bed.

I watched as he got comfortable. I loved that quality about him. He could get comfortable anywhere. I laid down beside him and played with his hair.

"Did you miss me?" He looked me in my eyes.

"The most." I nodded.

"One day, we're not going to need to hide. One day we're going to be together. Just me and you and a house full of pups. The impact you have on me is unlike anyone I've ever met." He smiled.

"What do you mean?" I smiled back.

"I could be having the worst day in the world but the minute I hear your voice or see your face, it all fades away. You're like a blanket of peace. I know things are hectic right now but I'm not going anywhere." He kissed me.

I laid my head on his chest and listened to the echoes of silence. There was no heartbeat. There was no sound of blood rushing through his veins, it was just peace. Peace within him, peace between us. I loved every minute of it until I dozed off.

When I woke up Owen was gone and Isis was changing her clothes.

"They left?" I frowned as I sat up.

"Yes but Owen said he'll be back. They went to go check on Sarai." She slipped on her skirt.

"Where are you going?" I yawned.

"To mingle, duh." She sat down on my bed. "Come."

"You're going to go meet new guys after mingling in the closet with Rowan?" I playfully judged her.

"Absolutely. Rowan and I are a casual thing." She shrugged.

"Does he know that?" I grabbed my bag from by my feet.

"Yes." She walked over to the mirror. "I think."

"What would they call beings like you in Veronica's movies?" I pretended to ponder. "Oh yeah, a skank."

"Such an ugly word." She admired herself. "Please come."

"I'd rather unpack." I opened my bag.

"So you'd rather be boring?" She taunted me.

"If that's what you want to call it." I shrugged as I unpacked.

"You want to spend our first night tucked off in our rooms?" She pulled me to my feet. "No way. If Sarai was here she'd want us to have the time of our lives. So let's do it. For her."

"I hate it when you guilt trip me." I slipped my shoes on.

"Yes!" She cheered.

"Let's go before I change my mind." I opened the door for her.

"You're the sweetest." She pinched my cheek.

We walked down the hallways and outside where a group of people were watching a live band play. There were booths set up all around with different logos on them. I watched everyone interact while I felt completely out of place.

"Isn't this great?" Isis linked arms with me.

"Yeah." I smiled.

"Let's go see what this worlds all about." She walked over to a booth that had the least people.

"Hello and welcome to Ridgeview. I'm Amy Strause." A tall brunette greeted us. "Interested in joining the MeshNet?"

"Uh, sure." Isis looked at me. "What's it about?"

"It's basically a friendship group with a secret society." She handed us a flyer.

"I've never heard of a friendship group." Isis looked at the paper.

"Of course you haven't." A blonde girl stepped in front of Amy.

"Not where you're from." She snatched the flyer.

"What's that supposed to mean?" Isis asked defensively.

"Back off, Jade." Amy pushed her back.

"No. They need to hear this if they plan on coming here and I'm glad to be the first of many to say it." She smiled insincerely.

A crowd slowly started to form around us. I stood beside Isis proudly.

"Say what?" Isis leaned on the table.

"You don't belong here." She whispered.

"Wanna come around the table and say that?" Isis challenged her.

"Actually-"

"Ladies, ladies, ladies." A guy intervened with his group of friends.

"That is enough heat. You're already hot enough." One of them joked.

"So corny." Isis rolled her eyes.

"I know another word that rhymes with that and it's what I'm feeling." He grinned.

"Like I was saying." Isis turned her attention back to Jade.

"Like I was saying, what are you doing later?" He flirted with her.

"Not you." She put her hand in his face.

"I like that." He smiled through her hand. "Names Eric."

"See ya." She rolled her eyes. "Let's go, Xena."

"Yeah, go Xena." Jade taunted me.

"Actually, let's sign up for the group. I want you to see my face everywhere you look." I grabbed the clipboard and wrote our names down. "See you when the semester starts, Bitch."

I pulled Isis away from the table and over to the fountain. We sat on the edge and talked about what just happened. Isis played hard to get but I knew she liked the attention.

"I like you when you're mean." Isis smiled. "I'll grab us two hot dogs."

"Yum." I watched her skip over to the stand.

"Hello." The girl sitting next to me waved.

She was tiny and her voice was the softest. Her hair was in a high ponytail and her glasses took up half her face. She was beautiful. You could tell she felt just out of place as I did.

"Hi." I waved back.

"You're Xena." She smiled.

"Yeah." I nodded awkwardly. "Do I know you?"

"No, but I know you." She slid closer to me. "I'm a witch too. I know your dad and I've seen your segment-"

"Let's not talk about that." I sighed. "But, you go here?"

"Yeah. I'm a junior." She smiled.

"Hey, who's this?" Isis handed me a hot dog.

"This is-"

"Kelsey Elmore." She reached to shake Isis' hand.

"Hello Kelsey." Isis met her reach. "You go here?"

"Yeah." She nodded bashfully. "I should get going but I'll see you guys around. My rooms right across from yours."

"See you around." I smiled.

"Bye." She walked away.

"You made a friend." Isis sat down next to me. "She's pretty."

"I know." I stared down at the hot dog.

"Oh just bite it." She forced it to my lips. "It's good."

I took a bite and fell in love. It was so good. Father would have a fit if he knew I was eating it which made me enjoy it even more.

"Look at us, being normal college students eating fattening foods and relaxing by the fountain." Isis indulged in her fantasy.

"Yeah." I played along.

"This could be us for real." She put her arm around me.

"Definitely." I smiled at her.

We spent the rest of the day as "normal college students" and Isis loved every minute of it. I really didn't care for the attractions but seeing her happy made it all worth while. I couldn't wait until we turned in for the night. I was truly exhausted. I climbed in bed and didn't say a word to Isis. She was too drunk off of cocktails to care.

I purposefully snoozed my first few alarms. I just wanted to sleep the days away. If Owen wasn't here, I didn't care to be. Truthfully I wanted to be in our room as much as possible in case he popped up. I didn't want to miss him.

My plan to sleep the day away was interrupted by Isis' loud singing in the shower. I just knew she already had the whole day planned in her head and I was 100% unprepared for it.

I pulled my phone from my duffle bag and checked to see if I had any messages from Owen. There was nothing from him. I scrolled through the other notifications and selected the facemail I never listened to.

"Hey it's me, Cat." Her face appeared. "I'm in trouble Xena. I can't explain it now but if anything happens, I love you. You'll see me soon. Stay close to V and Isis. They'll have your back in the end. Trust no one."

"What was that about?" Isis towel dried her hair.

"It was Catarina." I sighed.

"That's a strange message, right?" She looked at me.

"Yeah. I'm actually worried." I put the phone under my pillow.

"A lot of weird shit is going on lately." She shoved her toothbrush in her mouth.

"I'm not going anywhere today, don't even ask." I laid back in bed.

"Neither am I." She walked back into the bathroom.

"Knock knock." Someone said through the door.

"Who could that be?" Isis peeked her head around the corner.

"No clue." I slipped on my robe and opened the door.

"Hey, it's me Amy." She smiled. "I just wanted to say I'm sorry for how Jade treated you guys yesterday. Her moms the dean so she feels she has all the power. She got tipped off about your visit days ago. Just ignore her, I try to."

"Thank you." I smiled back.

"Yeah, that was really kind of you." Isis said behind me. "You can let her know that she's still a-"

"Bitch, yeah. I got it." She walked away.

"Well that was nice." I closed the door.

"Yeah." Isis smirked.

"So if we're not going out, what are we doing?" I grabbed my toothbrush.

"Spending quality time." She pulled her hair into a ponytail. "And we're going to start by you giving me every steamy detail of you and Owen in the office while I paint your nails."

"Anything but pink." I gave in.

We spent the day catering to ourselves. Painting our nails, face masks, venting. I told her everything that happened between Owen and I and she ate it up. Isis just loved hearing about other beings love lives especially the intimate parts. I just wanted the weekend to be over and it was only Saturday.

"Xena." Isis shook me awake. "Xena."

"Yeah?" I opened my eyes.

The moonlight shined on her face full of tears.

"We're in trouble." She cried. "They know something."

"Who?" I sat up.

"Our parents. Your dad is waiting outside for us. Get up." She grabbed her bag. "I packed your stuff too."

"What do they know?" I frantically slipped on my coat and shoes.

"I don't know!" She shouted. "But it has to be something for them to come get us. We can't even use our portal, we have to go with them."

"I'm scared." I started to hyperventilate.

"No. You can't do this right now. We have to go." She grabbed me by the arms.

"Okay." I ran out the door and over to the elevators.

My heart raced as we walked out the double doors. This was it. We were caught. Everything we did was for nothing. My reputation destroyed. I tried to do the right thing and I was about to be punished for the rest of my life.

"Xena." My father jumped out of the truck and charged at me.

"Father." I stepped back.

"Where is she?" He yelled.

"Who?" I glanced over at Isis.

"Isis, get in the car! This doesn't concern you!" He ordered her.

"Yes Sir." She ran to the car.

I tried to follow after her and he slung me back by my hair so hard it made my head spin.

"Where the hell is Sarai?" He snarled.

"I don't know!" I sobbed.

"You are the only being I told about her case! You think I'm idiotic?" He ran up in my face.

"I don't know where she is!" I screamed.

"You're a fucking liar! Get in the truck, now!" He grabbed me by coat and forced me in front of him.

I slid into the back next to Isis. She was bawling her eyes out. Father got in the front and slammed his door.

"Drive!" He ordered the man in the drivers seat.

I sat there thinking of the ways I could die while Isis sobbed the entire way. Father had never put his hands on me or yelled at me like that. I could see the veins in his neck and forehead. I could feel the rage radiating from his body. There was no turning back now.

No one said a word as we crossed back over into our dimension. I could tell Isis felt bad for me, and somehow, I felt worse for her. She was seeing what her beloved Godfather was capable of.

We walked into the house and my mother was waiting for us.

"Isis, not a word. Straight upstairs." My father spoke calmly. "Xena, stay right here."

Isis ran upstairs and slammed my door.

"If you're just going to berate me, please just take me straight to the council." I sat on the bottom stair.

"Xena, please." My mother sighed.

"Just when I thought we were getting somewhere." I shook my head.

"We're back to square one because you're never honest!" He hissed.

"Mother, he put his hands on me." I cried.

"You what?" She stepped between us.

"She's lying Azura! She knows something!" He roared.

"You need to go to your office!" She raised her voice. "This conversation is going nowhere tonight."

"No!" He charged towards me.

"Brice!" My mother slapped him.

Everything got extremely quiet. You could see the disbelief on my fathers face. She's never yelled at him let alone put her hands on him. I'd never seen either of them as upset as they were tonight.

"Go to your office or leave!" She walked over to the front door.

"Fine." He sighed. "I'll go to my office."

"Good." She watched him.

"This isn't over." He pointed at me before storming off.

"I love you Xena, goodnight." Mother ran up the stairs.

I just sat there. Afraid to move. Afraid to stay. I was frozen. I did this. I caused this tension between them. I put Sarai's family and Owen's in jeopardy. I keep making near sighted decisions and expecting different results. I literally knew better but did it anyway. Now we're all in situations we can't get out of.

I wanted to check on Isis and Mother but I wanted to listen in on my fathers conversation. I could hear his voice echoing down the halls.

I crept over to his door and listened closely.

"I'm sending her off." He bellowed. "No, I don't care. It has to be soon. Things went too far. She's up to something, I know it."

"Xena." Veronica whispered.

"Hold on." I whispered back.

"Yes, by tomorrow night she will be gone. I can't risk it. I have too much going for myself." He went on. "Yes, I'm leaving now."

I wanted to gather more information but Veronica needed me.

"X!" Isis leaned over the staircase.

"Coming." I sighed.

I tiptoed up the stairs and pulled her into my room.

"Are you okay?" We said at the same time.

"No." She hugged me.

"I know." I rubbed her back.

"That was so hard to watch. I hate him for you." She sobbed.

"He's trying to send me away, Isis. He really believes I did something with Sarai." I sat her down.

"Wait. Is he serious?" She sniffled. "He can't."

"He can." I pulled my necklace from my jewelry box.

"What are you doing with your pendant?" She wiped her tears.

"I'm leaving." I collected a few things from around my room and put them in a bag.

"You're just going to go?" Isis' tears stared flowing again.

"What other choice do I have? To wait until he ships me off somewhere? No thank you." I slung my bag over my shoulder.

I heard the dinging of the portal, Father was leaving again. Now was my chance.

"Give me a hug, I have to go." I opened my door.

She pulled me in and I didn't want to let go but I only had a limited time to pull this off without being tracked.

"I need to go find Veronica. I have to say bye." I ran down the stairs. "Veronica!"

"In here." She replied.

I could hear the dishes being washed. I walked into the kitchen and tried to fight my tears. This was going to be the hardest goodbye.

"V." I sobbed.

She was standing at the sink, her baby bump exposed.

"Yes." She turned to face me.

"Why are you-"

The expression on her face said it all. I could tell she had been crying. I rushed to her side.

"She knows." She cried.

"But how?" I grabbed a towel and dried her hands off.

"She went through my things and found vitamins for the baby." She sighed. "All those comments about me gaining weight I knew she was suspicious."

"So what now?" I glanced down at my wristwatch.

"She gave me two choices." She sat down. "Either she tells your father and I go to purgatory or I give her the baby."

"What? That's insane." I growled. "Here's a 3rd option, I'm running away. Come with me."

"You're running away? Where will you go?" She rubbed her stomach.

"Owen's. We can hide you there until we can get you to Dev." I promised her.

"But why are you going? Talk to me." She frowned.

"They think I have something to do with Sarai's disappearance." I confessed.

"Did you?" She stared at me.

"Don't ask me that right now. I don't want to lie to you." I sighed. "We don't have much time. Are you coming or not?"

"Yes and I'm already packed." She stood up. "I was planning on leaving too. I was just waiting for you to get home. I couldn't just leave you again."

"I'm going to go grab your contract. Meet me in the portal room." I headed for Fathers office.

"Xena." Isis pleaded. "Please don't leave me."

I ignored her pleas as I searched through my fathers' files. I grabbed Veronica's file and threw it in the fire.

"Stay!" She grabbed me.

"Come." I wiped her tears.

"I can't." Her voice broke.

"And I can't stay." I hugged her. "I gotta go. Go home."

"Here." I handed her my phone. "Destroy it. Say nothing. You know nothing."

She nodded and ran out crying.

When I got in the portal room, Veronica was already waiting for me. I closed and locked the door behind myself. I waited for the flashing blue lights before opening it again.

"Where are we exactly, Xena?" Veronica asked as we stepped out of the broom closet.

"We are in Owen's private office. This is the only address I had. I saw a piece of mail on his desk at BDSR." I pulled out my secret phone.

"What are you doing now?" She looked over my shoulder.

"I was going to call Owen but I shouldn't. It's too risky." I sighed. "Help me look for something with his home address."

"Okay." She walked over to his desk.

I started to pace back and forth as the reality of what we just done set in. I had no choice but to leave before Father did something drastic. I was so grateful that Veronica was here with me. We could face whatever together.

"I found something." She walked over to me.

"Okay. Lets try it." I led her back to the portal room. "Can you put the address in? I'm shaking."

"Of course." She walked over to the panel.

"Wait!" I stopped her. "I just remembered his condo is directly across the street."

We walked out the office and into the snow. We crossed the street and I knocked on the door. The butterflies in my stomach were now flooding my throat.

"Xi?" He opened the door. "What are you doing here?"

"I, uh. We-" I cried. "We had no other place to go."

"Welcome home." He embraced me.

Made in United States
North Haven, CT
02 July 2023

38469603R00108